Texas Fever

John Ewing has a dream. He wants to put defeat in the war behind him, and make something of his life. In his case, that means taking a herd of three thousand Texas Longhorns along the Chisholm Trail, all the way from San Antonio to the Kansas Pacific railhead in Abilene, Kansas. A dangerous journey of over seven hundred miles, with seemingly everything against him.

But he has far more to contend with than just hostile Indians, prejudice from the victorious northerners and nature itself. Vernon Peck, an old Confederate Army comrade, turns up out of nowhere in desperate need of a job. His lethal talent with a gun brings undoubted benefits, but is employment all he is really after? And in addition, transcending all other concerns, there is the one thing that could ruin all of Ewing's hopes . . . Texas Fever!

Texas Fever

Paul Bedford

A Black Horse Western

ROBERT HALE

© Paul Bedford 2019
First published in Great Britain 2019

ISBN 978-0-7198-3029-7

The Crowood Press
The Stable Block
Crowood Lane
Ramsbury
Marlborough
Wiltshire SN8 2HR

www.bhwesterns.com

Robert Hale is an imprint
of The Crowood Press

The right of Paul Bedford to be identified as
author of this work has been asserted by him
in accordance with the Copyright, Designs and
Patents Act 1988

CHAPTER ONE

The continuous lowing from thousands of Texas Longhorns seemed to fade into the background as the approaching rider suddenly claimed all of John Ewing's attention. Even after five years, he had no doubt at all about the newcomer's identity, and as a consequence the hairs seemed to lift on the back of his neck.

'Goddamn it,' he muttered. 'Why now, after all this time?'

Easing himself away from the chuck wagon's hinged counter, he carefully placed the mug of scalding coffee on it, and stood arms folded, waiting as the lone horseman drew closer. His eyes narrowed against the bright spring sunshine as he took in the other man's appearance. The hard features were as lean as ever, but definitely a little older. There were maybe slight flecks of grey in the gingery hair, but then again that could just as easily have been trail dust. What hadn't changed were the ever-watchful demeanour and hooded eyes that were now very definitely focused on him.

'See you're still favouring those Navy Sixes,' Ewing remarked evenly, as the individual he knew as Vernon Peck reined in before him.

His right hand gently caressing the nearest forward-facing revolver butt, Peck favoured him with the makings of a smile. 'They ain't embarrassed me yet,' he retorted softly, before raising his voice slightly. 'So how you doing, John? I ain't seen you since the surrender.'

Ewing sighed. He didn't care to be reminded of the late conflict. It was one reason why he had moved out west, albeit still in the south. Even now, some memories were still too raw. 'Lot's happened since then, Vern. I've gone into the cattle business. Kind of hoping to make some real money for a change.'

Peck glanced around, as though seeing the large herd for the first time. Beyond the chuck wagon there was an equally impressive hive of activity, as a glowing branding iron was applied to temporarily immobilised cattle, and wranglers worked at break-ing the spare horses that such an outfit would require. 'That's one hell of a lot of beef,' he remarked, before easing up out of his creaking saddle and dismounting. 'Where you fixing on taking it?'

For a moment Ewing remained silent, covering both surprise and unaccustomed uncertainty by scratching a bristly chin. There couldn't be anyone, anywhere in the south who hadn't heard of the great cattle drives, as cow men took their animals north to the railheads in Kansas. With Longhorns fetching merely four dollars each in Texas, but forty dollars and more from stock buyers like Joseph G. McCoy in Abilene, there was a big opportunity for men with grit and determination. So why would a man whom he had come to know so intimately feign ignorance about such a thing, unless there was some ulterior motive?

Again John Ewing sighed, and settled his penetrating gaze on the individual facing him. 'Just what brings you here, Vern? You running from somebody or something?'

As Peck laughed and shook his head, a sprinkling of dust cascaded from his well-worn plains hat. 'Five years since you clapped eyes on me, and I don't even get offered a cup of coffee. Seems a mite harsh . . . *considering.*'

Cowboys just loved nicknames, and the members of Ewing's crew were no different. 'Mesquite' Bill and 'Buckskin' Joe, although still only in their early twenties, were time-served drovers who worked well together. They made the branding of steers seem like child's play. Such was their skill that they could even observe events around them without slackening speed or misdirecting the red-hot iron as they applied the Bar E brand. Since they were now well used to the evocative sight of the Alamo Mission church's battered facade in the background, it was therefore the chuck wagon and its immediate environs that took their attention.

'That *hombre* must be something special to get a cup of coffee off of the boss,' Bill commented. 'He ain't even done anything yet and already he's getting considerations.'

Joe grunted, indicating his agreement and also the effort required to control the struggling animal beneath him. 'Maybe so, but God help him if he tries for a piece of pie. Cookie likes to be asked first, an' then still slap you down.' There was a brief silence followed by, 'Oh shit! Here we go.'

Peck's eyes lit up hungrily as he spotted the freshly baked apple pie. He had been existing on short commons for far too long. And, of course, such luxuries were only available while the outfit remained in San Antonio, with access to a wood-fired oven. Once on the trail, as he soon hoped to be, it would be bacon, biscuits and beans, with maybe some buffalo steaks if the drovers got lucky. So, reaching out with his left hand, the new arrival eagerly scooped out a sizeable chunk.

The razor-sharp blade slammed into a water barrel attached to the wagon, bare inches from Peck's head. His response was breathtaking in its speed and significance, and definitely took the cook by surprise. Instinctively dropping the coffee cup rather than the much-anticipated pie, he drew and cocked a Colt Navy in the mere blink of an eye. Even as its gaping muzzle sought out the owner of the knife, his forefinger tightened on the trigger. As pockmarked skin seemed to stretch taut over suddenly prominent cheekbones, his eyes glinted with palpable menace. Here was a very dangerous man!

Without hesitation, Ewing stepped directly in front of the revolver. 'You shoot my cook, an' there'll be thirty hungry men after your blood,' he stated flatly. 'And I'll be one of them, because we're fixing to move out tomorrow. If he'd intended to cut you, you'd be bleeding already.'

For long seconds, the two men stared at each other, until Peck drew in a deep breath and allowed the tension to abate. Nevertheless, Ewing stayed put until the Colt had been holstered. Only then did he step aside and allow the two protagonists to view each other.

Short, stocky and considerably older than the rest of the men, Nico Montoya hailed from Sonora, but his parentage was a mixture of Anglo and Mexican. Fiery blood still flowed through his veins, but it was not so hot that he couldn't recognize that he had very likely had a lucky escape. This new man bore the mark of a born killer, and was obviously someone to step well clear of. And yet . . . earning sixty dollars a month meant that Nico the Cook felt entitled to some respect.

'Anybody wants something from me, they ask first. *Sí?*'

Vernon Peck regarded him silently. He had no love for ' 'breeds' or 'greasers' at the best of times, and especially not one that threatened him with an Arkansas Toothpick. But then he became aware of Ewing's eyes boring into him, and he recalled that if things went according to plan he would be eating from this chuck wagon for maybe the next two months. 'Yeah, yeah,' he finally responded brusquely, before turning away and filling his mouth with the purloined pie.

John Ewing placed a hand on his old army comrade's back, and gently but firmly propelled him out of earshot. It was time for some straight talking. 'I'll ask you again, Vern. Just what brings you here?'

That man sighed, but continued to munch on the delightful pastry for a while as he marshalled the appropriate words. 'Goddamn, but that was good,' he ultimately replied before continuing with, 'Well I'll tell you, John, things ain't exactly been rosy since Appomattox. I've drifted here an' there, an' done some things I probably shouldn't have. Truth is, I ain't found it easy to settle on anything decent. What I need right now is a job, an' regular vittles to put some meat back on these bones. So when I heard in Gonzales that a certain John Ewing was looking for trail hands, I thought I'd chance my luck an' take a ride over here.'

The trail boss, for that was now his role in life, regarded Peck with mixed feelings. Gonzales was over seventy miles away, and he knew no one in that town. It was a sad fact that even when they were watching each other's backs, during General Lee's interminable forced marches, Ewing had felt that he could never entirely trust his lethal friend. And yet, there could be no denying that he owed this man a great debt . . . as he was about to be reminded.

'Saving your miserable hide at Chancellorsville must count for something,' Peck chided gently.

Ewing coloured slightly. That had been a cheap shot, but nonetheless it turned the tide. 'OK, OK. You're hired. Thirty dollars a month and found. And any cartridges you use to defend the herd. A man with your particular . . . *talents* might could come in useful if we come up agin any hostile Indians.'

'I didn't know there was any other kind,' his new employee retorted coolly.

Ewing's expression suddenly hardened. 'You need to know that I won't tolerate any trouble on this drive. There'll be no drinking and no gambling. Anyone kills another man on the trail, he'll be tried and hung by the rest of us. And take my advice. Don't make an enemy of the cook, or you could find yourself shitting for fun.'

That was just too much for Peck. Even the Army of Northern Virginia hadn't made so many demands on him. In a loud voice, he remarked, 'Well if I *do* get sick, I'll know exactly who to go for!'

Ewing chose to ignore that, because he had one more rule to announce, which he felt sure would raise the other man's hackles. 'One last thing. Before we leave here, every man stores his gun-belt in the chuck wagon. And unless we get big trouble on the way, they stay there until you get paid off at the railhead. That way, arguments between young hotheads can't turn into gunplay.'

It was Peck's turn to colour up. 'You got to be goddamn joshing me.'

'Do I look like I am?'

'So what do we use for killing snakes an' such?'

Ewing shook his head in disbelief. 'Always it's the snakes. What has everyone got against the god-damned things?' Before the other man could answer, he quickly continued, 'If it's sport you're after, beat them with sticks. But if you've just got to shoot them, use your long guns.'

An unmistakeable chill came over the newcomer. It was very apparent that he saw nothing humorous about this particular rule. 'I don't take my guns off for any man,' he snarled.

The cattleman shrugged and affected indifference. 'Well then, you won't be working for this outfit, Vern. Because that's just the way it is. For everyone, including me. Take it or leave it!'

Peck drew in his second, steadying breath since dismounting, and then blew out through his nose like a horse. 'What the hell's come over you, John? You're all shit an' no sugar now. You never used to be this straight-laced. You got religion or something?'

This time Ewing was genuinely unmoved. 'Responsibilities. That's what I've got. I'm taking more than three thousand head and thirty some men across Texas, fording more rivers than you could shake a stick at. Then up through the Indian Territory and into Kansas. That's well over seven hundred miles as the crow flies. Only the thing is, cattle ain't crows, so like as not we've got at least two months eating dust. And I don't want to reach Abilene and have to think back on all the graves we've dug. So it's done my way, or not at all. You in or out?'

Vernon Peck viewed his old comrade-in-arms afresh. Without doubt, John Ewing had changed. He'd changed a heck of a lot, and not necessarily for the best. But at the end of the day, needs must. Which, of course, meant eating not only apple pie but also humble pie . . . for the present. And so, mustering the makings of a smile, he replied, 'Oh what the hell. I reckon I'm for signing on, *boss*.'

CHAPTER TWO

For the nearby residents of San Antonio de Bexar it must have sounded as though all hell had broken loose, but thankfully on this occasion Comanche warriors were not to blame. As the new day dawned, a tremendous chorus of 'Yeehaas' and assorted yells suddenly split the air, and the great, extended herd began to move. Only slowly at first, because the well-fed cattle had grown used to their surroundings, along with the plentiful grazing that the arrival of spring had created.

Until Peck's unexpected arrival, Ewing had taken on thirty drovers, working on the basis that ten men were required to control one thousand cattle. In addition, he employed three wranglers, whose task was to manage the remuda of spare mounts. The drovers, most of whom were slim and wiry, because big men were too hard on horses, moved into the positions dictated by their experience or lack of it. The top hands were assigned to point and swing duty, which meant front and flanks respectively. The least knowledgeable came up at the rear, and so were doomed to quite literally eating dust. Vernon Peck, with little prior knowledge of controlling steers, was one of those unfortunates.

Despite all the noisy activity, it was only when the mule team hauling the chuck wagon was urged into motion that the drive was deemed to have truly begun, because now the all-important food source was on the move. And, as the inexperienced would likely discover, this conveyance often satisfied more than just their hunger. Along with the more usual staples, it also carried coal oil to combat lice, and bison tallow, which when combined with salt was considered to be a useful treatment for piles.

Nico Montoya immediately took up a position on the left flank, well clear of the choking dust. As he glanced back and observed the newest recruit's obvious discomfort, his lips curled in a wry smile. It never occurred to him to wonder why such a *hombre duro* would tolerate this kind of work in the first place. All he did know was that the contentious apple pie was long gone, and there would be no more for months.

The indispensable chuck wagon was followed by another less elaborate wagon, and one that was relatively new to trail drives. On the early trips north, calves born on the journey had been regarded as an impediment, and so were quickly killed. Then it was realized that if the creatures survived, they would be worth cash money at the railhead, and so outfits began to procure a second wagon and its accompanying teamster.

John Ewing had attended to some last-minute business in San Antonio, and so came up at the rear of the great departure. Viewing the vast expanse of moving flesh, he slowed his mount to allow time for some unaccustomed reflection. This would most likely be the only occasion on the drive when he might be relatively carefree. If he could have known just how true that was to be, he would probably have tarried a great deal longer. As it was, it suddenly dawned on him that this enterprise was only finally happening because of his efforts, and he felt a tremendous surge of pride. After the wasted years of war and its sad aftermath, something positive was actually occurring in his life. For long moments, the trail boss took a last look at his adopted home town until, catching sight of his old comrade, a broad smile spread across his features.

Urging his horse over to join the hunched figure, Ewing called out, 'How's it going, Vern? Enjoying your first cattle drive?'

That man slowly glanced around. Even with a bandanna pulled up over his nose and mouth, there was no mistaking the sour expression. 'Christ!' he exclaimed. 'This is worse than getting shot at by Yankees. Why the hell d'you need someone back here anyhu? The goddamned cows are all going that away. And why me in particular? I've never done you any wrong . . . that you know of,' he added, with a weak attempt at humour.

Ewing grunted, and then gestured for Peck to follow him, away from the herd. A short while later, and just as the latter individual gratefully lowered his bandanna, the two of them watched as a couple of steers began to drift away from the main group.

'Because you really are dealing with dumb animals,' the cattleman explained. 'If you're not watching them all the time, you'll suddenly find that a bunch of them have just wandered off. And then we've lost the equivalent of a few men's wages.'

Peck held up his hands in submission. 'OK, OK, *boss.* I get the picture.'

But his new employer wasn't finished with him just yet. 'And the reason you've pulled this shit duty, is because you're new to all this. Someone's got to do it, and you've got to learn. There can't be any favourites on this trip, Vern. It's too important.'

Peck regarded him intently, as though he suddenly had more on his mind. 'This herd. Is it really all yours? Just don't seem possible, is all.'

Ewing thoughtfully returned the gaze. He wasn't used to fielding questions from his employees, but then again this man wasn't just another hand. 'No. No it ain't. About a third of it's mine. Those with the Bar E brand on them. The rest belong to various ranchers in these parts. With the Comanches acting up an' all, they didn't want to leave their families. I agreed to act as trail boss on wages, to drive them all to Abilene. Once all the hands, including me, have been paid off, I split what's left with the other owners. Having said that, whilst on the trail I consider them all to be mine. Anyone tries to steal them, they're stealing *my* cattle!'

Peck whistled in amazement. Minor details didn't interest him, just the end result. And he possessed brains enough to do the ciphers. 'That'll amount to a shit load of dinero. These other fellas back in Texas must *really* trust you.'

'They do,' Ewing retorted sharply. 'Which is why I don't intend letting them down, and why *everyone* needs to pull their weight. So get that bandanna back over your face, and round up those two steers before more of them decide to wander off.'

For a brief moment, something flashed dangerously in Peck's eyes, before disappearing just as quickly as he regained control. Flicking a mock salute, he remarked, 'Sure thing, boss,' before swinging his mount away.

Ewing observed the retreating figure with mixed emotions. There was something about Vernon Peck that made him twitchy . . . but then hadn't that always been the case?

The first night out of San Antonio passed completely devoid of incident. Lightning was without doubt the biggest cause of stampedes, but the sky was mercifully clear and unthreatening. Every man was expected to take his turn guarding the herd. It had been discovered that any standard of gentle singing soothed the animals, and so that too was required of those on duty, as they slowly circled the herd in opposite directions. Then, all too soon for many of the sleeping young men, indications of daylight arrived and Montoya was serving up hot coffee and beans.

Then, in a routine that would become all too familiar, John Ewing called out, 'Saddle up, boys. We're burning daylight,' and the whole outfit found itself on the move again.

The route that the Bar E cattle were to follow was by then a well-used one known as the Chisholm Trail, blazed years earlier by a half-breed Cherokee trader to move his goods around trading posts. Now indelibly worn into the landscape from years of employment, it was still the most favoured route up into Kansas. As far as rivers were concerned, it wouldn't have mattered which trail that Ewing had chosen, because there were just so damn many of them. And the first one to be crossed, late that afternoon, was the Guadalupe, so named by a seventeenth-century Spanish explorer.

The man on point, as they approached it, went by the name of Reno. He knew his job, otherwise he wouldn't have been there, and yet it didn't require any experience to recognize that they'd got a big problem. And one that was nothing to do with the depth of the water.

'Savages in the trees on the far side of the river, Mister Ewing,' the drover reported breathlessly. 'Comanches or Kiowas, I reckon.'

That man grimaced. Barely twenty-five miles from San Antonio, and already they'd hit trouble. 'How many?'

'Enough to stop us crossing if they choose to.'

'Damn, damn, damn,' Ewing intoned. 'We sure could have done without this.'

19

The news spread down the line like wildfire until it reached Vernon Peck. Still riding drag, he actually welcomed anything that might take him from his loathsome task. And he reckoned that hostile Indians were as good an excuse as any to abandon his post. Yanking down the bandanna, he urged his mount over to the chuck wagon. Montoya regarded him curiously.

'I've got a gunbelt and two Colt Navys in back of this thing,' Peck announced. 'I need them, *now*.'

The cook's eyes widened. He didn't choose to take instructions from some two-bit drover, however tough he might seem. 'Not without Mister Ewing's say so,' he replied firmly.

As before, the skin seemed to tighten over Peck's cheekbones, and this time a flush of colour came to them. Suddenly reaching down to his rifle scabbard, he withdrew a 'Yellow Boy' Winchester, levered in a cartridge and pointed the muzzle directly at Montoya's belly.

'The last time I gut shot someone, he was days dying. I guess it would have been a terrible sight to see . . . if I could have given a damn. Now hand me my pistolas, old man. Pronto!'

Ewing, Reno and a couple of others reined in on the Guadalupe's south bank. Sure enough, the oak trees on the far side were swarming with Indians. If the drovers were to force a crossing with the herd, there would likely be a lot of dying, and mostly on their side.

'You reckon they're looking for a fight, boss?' Reno nervously enquired.

Ewing was no Indian fighter, but he possessed plenty of common sense. 'Nah. If this was a murder raid, I reckon they'd have hit us already. I think they're just hoping for some easy pickings.' Since he had more important things to spend money on than fancy firearms, it was an old Spencer that he eased out of its leather scabbard, as he added, 'Seems like time for a parley.'

Yet before he could make a move towards the river, there came the sound of shod hoofs behind him. 'You ain't figuring on treating with them savages, are you?' Peck demanded.

Ewing turned to view the dust-coated figure. He couldn't fail to notice that the other man had his Colts strapped on again. 'You got a better idea?'

Peck regarded him speculatively. 'Well yeah, actually I have. What you need is an ace in the hole.'

'You being the ace?'

'Uhuh,' the reluctant drover agreed. 'Makes sense that I do what I'm good at. So while you have a palaver, I cross over further down the river and come round behind them. If they're fixing on getting too greedy, I'll drop a few of them dirt worshippers for you. Show them you're not to be messed with. How's that sound?'

'Sounds kind of risky to me,' Ewing retorted dubiously.

'If you recall, it's what I was good at . . . back in the day.'

The cattle boss sighed. He was out to make money, not kill folks . . . even if they *were* Comanches! And yet he couldn't gainsay that Peck knew his business, and that it wouldn't hurt to be prepared. 'OK. Get into position. But no shooting unless I signal. If those sons of bitches will accept a few steers to leave us alone, then I'll go along with it. You understand me?'

'Oh, I understand you all right,' Peck answered obliquely, before quickly turning away and heading east.

Ewing stared after him in silence for a few moments, before turning to the others. 'You fellas stay here and cover me with your long guns. I'm gonna see if we can settle this peaceably.' With that, he levered up a cartridge from the cylindrical magazine in the Spencer's stock, and cocked the hammer. Then, canting the carbine across the saddlehorn, he eased his animal forward.

As the trail boss somewhat nervously approached the shallow riverbank, six warriors daubed with ochre and other more garish colours rode out from the cover of the trees. Others remained partially concealed under fresh spring foliage. Emanating primitive menace, this was a sizeable war party. At the sight of them, his heart began to beat like an anvil strike. Although having lived in Texas for three years, this was his first encounter with the frontier state's fiercest native inhabitants, and their appearance gave him no comfort whatsoever. All the tales of their bloody depredations came flooding back to him.

As the warriors stared implacably at him across the stretch of fast-flowing water, Ewing realized that it was up to him to open the negotiations. Except that he had no idea what to say. He certainly didn't speak Comanche, and presumably they didn't speak American. Draping the reins over his Spencer, he raised his left hand in greeting. The response, when it came, was not what he had been expecting, but proved that these savages were well used to extortion.

Without saying a word, one of them pointed directly at the approaching herd, and then raised two clenched fists. Swiftly, he opened and closed them five times. Fifty cattle! The son of a bitch expected a present of fifty steers in exchange for passage across the Guadalupe.

'The hell with that!' Ewing instinctively flung back, as he shook his head emphatically. His left hand was still raised in greeting, and so he rapidly clenched and extended his fingers twice in succession. A counter offer of ten animals. The question was, had he just insulted the Comanches, or merely demonstrated his willingness to haggle?

Vernon Peck felt some old feelings coming back to him, as always happened before the onset of brutal, bloody violence. They consisted of a strange mix of nausea and exhilaration. Yet, from past experience, he knew that they wouldn't affect his performance. He had crossed the Guadalupe without being observed, and was approaching the grove of trees where the Comanches lurked. He already had his left-hand Colt drawn and cocked, and as he got within reasonable pistol range he swiftly wrapped the reins around the saddlehorn and drew the other. He had long before mastered the art of controlling his horse with his legs alone, which was a good thing because he fully intended getting right in amongst the thieving savages. As far as he was concerned, Ewing's negotiations were just a smokescreen to obscure the onset of his bloodletting. From the higher ground behind the oaks, Peck could see a fair amount of gesticulation taking place. He grunted. Treating with Indians of any tribe was just a piece of foolishness. All they were fit for was killing. And so, dropping down the bank into the trees, he began to do just that.

There were maybe a dozen partially concealed warriors awaiting the outcome of the stilted parley, and none of them had considered the possibility of an attack from the rear. Consequently, Peck achieved total surprise. All he needed was an absence of mis-fires. Drawing a bead on his first victim, he seemed to hear the disconnected voice of his old commanding officer bawling out an oft-used decree. 'Powder burn the bastards!' Then he squeezed the trigger, and the carnage began.

The .36 calibre soft lead ball smashed into the back of a bronzed skull, flattening out as it did so, and then exiting in a mass of bone fragments and gore. For a few vital moments everything was confu-sion, and Peck took full advantage. Twisting slightly to avoid a tree trunk, he fired his other revolver at a warrior who was turning towards the unexpected threat. He too was struck in the head, and toppled from his pony without a sound. *Ten chambers remaining!*

The pistol fighter knew that to maintain the pressure, he had to keep burrowing into them like an Alabama tick. Urging his horse deeper into the trees, Peck rapidly tilted his Colts, so that when he cocked them any copper remnants of the used percussion caps fell clear of the cylinder mechanisms. Now very alive to the danger, one of the Comanches snapped off an ill-judged shot. Although this slammed harmlessly into timber, the white man knew that he wouldn't have everything his own way for much longer. It was time to push his luck.

Screaming like a berserker, he advanced between two warriors, and with consummate skill aimed and fired at both simultaneously. One Comanche, agonisingly gut shot, fell sideways and disappeared from view. The other took a ball in his chest that rocked him backwards. The muzzle had been so close that scorch marks from the powder flash were visible around the bloody wound. *Eight chambers remaining!*

With acrid smoke drifting through the trees, accompanied by howls of pain, the surviving warriors were unsure as to the number of their assailants. A superstitious fear of the unknown, compounded by an inherent unwillingness to take casualties, meant that they began to drift towards their companions by the river. Peck instinctively sensed that this was the tipping point. With two fresh chambers under a hammer, he again shifted position and opened fire. The cap'n ball revolvers recoiled satisfyingly in his hands. In an indication of their fear, both of his next victims were shot in the back. Bizarrely, they both toppled sideways off their ponies in opposite directions. *Six chambers remaining!*

Those last casualties effectively broke any remaining resolve. The surviving Comanches streamed out of the trees in terror, almost colliding with the startled warriors at the water's edge. They in turn were infected by the panic. All except their leader, who bellowed accusingly across the water, whilst at the same time raising his rifle.

John Ewing was taken aback by the turn of events, but had no choice other than to defend himself. Taking swift aim at the largest target with his Spencer, he sent a heavy bullet into the pony's chest, causing it to rear up and throw its rider. The warrior hit the grassy slope and rolled uncontrollably down to the water's edge. Quite amazingly, he had somehow retained his grip on the rifle and, although somewhat shakily, again attempted to draw a bead on the white man.

'I never wanted this,' Ewing yelled, but nevertheless levered up another cartridge. This time he took concerted aim at the chief, if indeed he was such, and squeezed off a well-considered shot. The heavy bullet slammed the Comanche back into the riverbank, snuffing out his life in an instant. And then, as quickly as it had started, the fight was all over. Those

Indians that could, fled to the north, leaving their dead and wounded to the cattlemen's tender mercies. In an amazingly one-sided encounter, no white men had even been injured.

Vernon Peck appeared out of the tree line and, his blood well and truly up, he screamed after the retreating Comanches. 'Run, you painted curs. And stay well clear of my cattle!'

Ewing stared at him in disbelief, but before he could say anything, the other man dismounted and strode back into the trees. With his revolvers cocked, it was brutally obvious what was in the offing. Sure enough, a few moments later, more gunshots crashed out. Some might have described them as mercy killings, but for Peck it was just a simple matter of tying up loose ends. And throughout the whole gory business, he knew exactly how many shots that he had left. Finally reappearing in the open, he mounted up and slowly made his way across the river. Spots of fresh blood were dotted about on his worn clothing.

'Well at least we know it's shallow enough here abouts,' he remarked casually, as he reined in next to his employer.

That man angrily shook his head. 'There was no need for all them killings. They would have accepted a few animals and gone on their way. We just had to reach an agreement, is all. Now, after what you've done, they might go find some friends and come back for blood.'

'What you getting all wrathy about?' Peck

demanded. 'Instead of giving away some valuable steers, you're a few ponies to the good. That's a fine outcome if you ask me. And as for them fellas coming back . . . well, that just ain't gonna happen. I heard tell that Comanches can't abide taking casualties. Makes them think that their medicine has turned bad.' He paused for a moment and favoured his old army buddy with a sly glance. 'But just in case I'm wrong, I'm keeping these Colts strapped on. It's up to you what you tell the rest of your crew.'

Ewing's body tensed as he recognized the unmistakable challenge. 'And what if I don't agree to that?'

Peck shrugged and smiled, but no warmth spread to his eyes. 'I'm too good with these for you to try and take them off me. And we ain't in San Antonio any more. This here's dangerous country.'

John Ewing sighed. So it was like that, was it? Briefly he contemplated his options. Despite Peck's proficiency with firearms, the trail boss wasn't afraid of him. Up close as they were, he could quite easily have knocked him out of his saddle and disarmed him. But that would have severely strained their friendship. And it was a fact that a man with his lethal abilities would still to be an asset where they were going, if he could be bridled a little. There was also the uncomfortable but undeniable truth that Ewing did still owe him his life. Drawing in a deep breath, he allowed the tension in his body to abate.

'Since when did you know so much about Comanches, anyhu?' he asked in a deliberately far lighter tone.

The gunhand, because really that was what he was, shrugged. 'Since I made it my business to find out. And now, I reckon I'd better make sure the whole herd hasn't disappeared through the back door, or you'll be chewing me out for that as well.' With that, he swung his mount away and headed back to his designated position in drag.

As John Ewing watched him ride off, an uncomfortable thought came to him. When taunting the fleeing Comanches, Peck had referred to the herd as '*my* cattle'. Was that a slip of the tongue in the heat of the moment, or something far more sinister?

CHAPTER THREE

John Ewing had pondered long and hard on whether to hold the herd back for a time, to see if any other threats materialised. The urge to seek advice from Reno, an experienced top hand, was almost overwhelming, but reluctantly he recognized that the decision had to be his alone. Very conscious that the eyes of many of his men were on him, the trail boss knew that he had to demonstrate his abilities as a leader. And so, with the horizon apparently clear in all directions, he finally signalled for the crossing to begin.

After a day on the move, the cattle needed no encouragement to take to the cool water. And once in, it took all the drovers' efforts to urge them out again, but too much liquid too quickly could do the animals' real harm. With the herd spread out over two miles, the sun was falling in the west before the final stragglers emerged on the north bank. Because of Peck's inexperience, Ewing had temporarily assigned Jase Spooner, a seasoned hand, to partner him at the rear.

As they ensured that no steers had been left behind, the two men carried out a quick sweep of the south bank. The lure of water had obviously been strong, because they didn't find a single creature. Not that Spooner really had cows on his mind. Suddenly very aware that most everyone else had crossed over, he was feeling particularly vulnerable.

'I just hope we've seen the last of them Comanches,' the young man muttered nervously. 'I surely do. You must have some nerve, taking them on the way you did.' Even as he spoke, his eyes flitted onto the Colts strapped to his companion's waist. He for one didn't resent the fact that they were still in place.

Peck favoured him with a half smile. 'Learnt my trade in the late war, just like your boss. Guess I just took to it better than most, is all. It's a fact that killing folks don't come hard to me.' His head tilted slightly, as he measured the uneasy reaction to that last statement. 'So what say we get across that damn river. I'm so hungry I could spit roast and eat that greaser cook of ours.'

Spooner's eyes bugged, but nevertheless he had to laugh at the novel thought. This new drover certainly was a strange one. There was something frighteningly chilling about him, and yet he couldn't deny that he was glad to have him around.

As the two horsemen approached the water, Spooner held back. 'You go over first,' he called out. 'I want to be able to say I was the last man across the

Guadalupe.' Suddenly realizing just how childish that must have sounded, he added somewhat self-consciously, 'It'll read out good, when I can pay someone to write a letter to my ma.'

Peck shrugged and rode on. He didn't even know if his ma was still alive. More to the point, he didn't care! After watering his horse in the waist high-river, he urged it up onto the north bank. Ahead was the tail end of the herd, but he wasn't in any all fired hurry to start eating dust again, and so he turned to watch the youngster across.

As his temporary partner had done, Jase Spooner allowed his mount to drink a reasonable amount whilst he enjoyed the tranquillity of the moment. Yet, as he glanced around, something strange upstream caught his eye. There were the usual ripples of the water's flow, but there was something else as well. As dreadful realization dawned, a chill totally uncon-nected to the water temperature raced through his body.

'Jesus Christ. Them's snakes,' he howled in panic. Desperately, he kicked his horse into reluctant motion. The north bank wasn't that far away, but some dreadful premonition told him they weren't going to make it.

From his position higher up, Peck could easily make out the twisting serpents, as they moved with the current and closed in on horse and rider. 'Get the hell out of there, kid,' he bellowed. 'Those ain't just any snakes. They're water moccasins!'

With the venomous creatures barely yards away,

Spooner grabbed his rifle, so as to beat at them, but that would be like trying to hit smoke. 'Shoot them!' he screamed at his companion.

Peck didn't even trouble to draw a revolver. There wasn't a cat in hell's chance of him hitting anything, and he wasn't one to waste powder. All he could do was watch with a certain gruesome fascination as the snakes lunged at their target. Spooner had drawn his legs up out of the stirrups, and so they went for the far easier bulk of his horse. As three separate sets of razor-sharp teeth bit into its body, the poor beast screamed in agony and charged for the bank. Naturally not realizing that frantic movement would only drive the poison around its system and so hasten its demise, the animal powered up out of the water in a desperate bid to escape the pain.

Terrified at the thought of being thrown backwards into the river, its rider rammed his boots back into the stirrups . . . which sadly turned out to be his undoing. Still clutching his rifle, and mounted on an uncontrollably frenzied creature, the shaken young drover struggled to stay in the saddle. Although they were now out of the water, he was far from safe. Because, as the horse's limbs spasmed, it unexpectedly bucked and he fell sideways. It would have been far better if he had been thrown completely clear, but his left boot remained stubbornly in the stirrup. Now completely helpless, Spooner was brutally dragged at speed across the hard ground. With the wind knocked out of his body, he couldn't even cry out.

Vernon Peck coolly weighed his options. To simply do nothing would be unseemly, but he sure didn't fancy chasing a runaway horse all over God's creation. Yet left to his own devices, the helpless trail hand could be towed for miles. Grunting, Peck pulled out his Winchester, levered in a cartridge and took swift aim. Firing twice in rapid succession, he brought the frenzied animal crashing down. It was only by pure happenstance that it didn't land on top of its suffering owner. As it was, Spooner was wrenched sharply to one side, and ended up lying half on, half off the twitching creature. His left leg, still caught up, had assumed a wholly unnatural angle that hinted at great trouble ahead.

John Ewing's first thought, when he heard the shooting, was that the goddamned Comanches had returned. Cursing volubly, he unsheathed his Spencer, and then bellowed at Montoya to hand back the gun belts to any that wanted them. Next he peered around, searching for the expected threat. Strangely, all he could see was a single animal on its side, back near the river. Then Peck came into view, holding his rifle, and Ewing's initial alarm began to subside. Perhaps they weren't under attack after all.

The trail boss, followed by a few drovers, cantered over to the dying horse, and to his dismay discovered Jase Spooner's twisted frame. The young man, battered and bleeding, was apparently still breathing but unconscious. 'What the hell happened?' he demanded of Peck, as that man joined them.

'Water moccasins bit his horse in the river. Damn

thing lit out like a Kentucky thoroughbred. All I could do was bring it down.'

Ewing glanced at him thoughtfully for a moment, before calling out to the nearest drover. 'Go tell Sam to fetch his wagon back here. This boy's gonna need some doctoring.' Only after that individual had galloped off did he say what was really on his mind. 'He could have been crushed to death, if this poor beast had fallen the other way.'

Peck didn't care for the inference. 'Better that than being dragged across the whole State of Texas. He's lost plenty of flesh as it is. Oh, an' you owe me for another two cartridges.'

Ewing's eyes narrowed, but he didn't rise to that. Because unfortunately, he had more important matters to think about.

'The cuts and bruises will heal in time, but it'll take more than any prickly pear poultice to fix this. Bone's broke bad below the knee,' Sam remarked sadly. Acting as teamster on the spare wagon, he had some knowledge of tending to calves and other critters, and so probably knew as much as anyone on the drive about such matters. 'I can surely splint the leg, but I can't answer for what'll become of him if it chooses to infect.'

Spooner lay on a blanket next to the campfire. His left leg was indeed a bloody mess. Having been liberally dosed with whiskey, which Montoya insisted had been brought along for purely medicinal purposes, he had finally drifted off into a fitful slumber.

'Damn, damn, damn,' Ewing intoned for the second time that day. Darkness had fallen, and the herd had been halted for the night. Moving off to the chuck wagon to eat his fill, his mind was a seething morass. Only two days on the trail and already they'd got a man hurt bad, and been in a fight with Comanches. That train of thought brought him around to Vernon Peck. He seemed to have been the catalyst for all the violence that day. And yet he couldn't really be blamed for any of the outside influences that had come into play. Killing things just happened to be what he excelled at!

It was as the trail boss finished his three 'B's', bacon, beans and biscuits, that Reno hunkered down next to him. The point man was the nearest thing Ewing had to a 'ramrod' in his outfit. Sandy haired and good-looking, he was quiet and thoughtful. And it was obvious that he had been pondering on Spooner's situation . . . amongst other things.

'However it turns out for Jase, he ain't gonna be any more use on this drive. Why don't you get Sam to take him back to the sawbones in San Antonio, boss? Without the herd to slow him up, he could be there and back in a day.'

Ewing smiled grimly. 'Oh, I'd like to. I truly would. But what if those damn Comanches are still in the area? Watching and waiting. One man and a cripple in a wagon wouldn't stand a chance against those devils. And I can't spare half a dozen men as an escort. This herd means too much to too many people, for me to take risks with it.'

Reno glanced carefully around the camp before continuing. 'You could spare *one* particular man. And he's likely all the escort that Sam would need. And we sure could do without him . . . for a day, that is.'

Despite the situation, Ewing chuckled. Knowing exactly who was doing what meant that he didn't need to check for a particular earwigger. Peck and another hand were working their stints as 'night hawks' around the herd. 'Sounds like you've taken agin my newest recruit.'

Reno sighed. He recognized that he could well be treading dangerously. 'I don't even know him, but I can recognize trouble when I see it. In spades!'

Ewing stared long and hard at the other man, before finally nodding. He accepted that Reno had no axe to grind, and was only expressing an honest opinion. And yet. . . .

'There's more than enough happened today already,' the trail boss decided. 'I'll sleep on it.' The air of finality indicated that nothing more would be said on the subject that night.

Although still dark, the announcement of breakfast meant that a new day had officially begun. With the expected and soon to be habitual grumbling, the hands packed up their bedrolls and brought themselves to life with heavily sugared coffee. Thankfully, the night had passed peacefully, with no trouble from either humans or the weather. Even Jase Spooner had slept through it, although the task of lifting him into Sam's wagon made every one realize just how badly his leg had been broken. The fearful noise that he made prompted Ewing into acting on the decision that he had come to.

Drifting over to Peck, he remarked, 'Young Spooner is finished on this drive. So I need you to escort him and Sam in the wagon back to San Antonio. That way he'll be decently treated, and you get to pass a day without eating trail dust. In fact, nothing would be said about it if you were to take a sip of bug juice while you were in town. How's that sound?' If Ewing had expected him to be pleased by such considerations, then he was about to be sadly disabused.

Peck sipped coffee and favoured him with a strangely side-long glance for a moment before sharply replying. 'Send someone else. I signed on as a drover, not a goddamned nursemaid.'

Ewing was taken aback. 'I choose to send you. There might be Comanches out there, and I reckon out of all of us you'd be best able to handle them.'

Peck sneered insolently, but what he said next proved that his mind was as honed as his tongue. 'My hide is worth more than any amount of gut rot whiskey, John Ewing. I came out on top yesterday because I got the drop on those painted sons of bitches in the trees. If a Comanche war party catches us out in the open, with a wagon that can't outrun them, we'll be dead meat for sure. An' it ain't my fault that that kid got himself set on by serpents. So I'll say it agin. I ain't going!' With that, he tossed the coffee dregs into the fire and calmly walked away.

Ewing blinked, as though waking from a bad dream. He couldn't believe what had just happened. His heart began to thump, as he realized that some of his men were watching him intently ... and waiting. Waiting to see if he took the newest employee to task. Cursing himself for a fool, he belatedly wished that he had taken Peck to one side before issuing his orders. But then he had never expected to be rebuffed. As it was, he had been made to look a fool in front of the other hired hands. And yet ... perhaps he should have thought his plan through more carefully, rather than just accept Reno's suggestion. Because Peck's refusal *had* contained a certain harsh logic that was hard to refute.

Turning, he stalked over to the chuck wagon's counter and plonked his mug down hard. Montoya's eyes briefly met his, and the cook offered him a warm smile. That individual had seen enough of life to understand what had just taken place, and to recognize the dilemma that beset his boss.

'Goddamn it all to hell,' Ewing muttered, before turning to face the camp. 'We're burning daylight,' he announced, even though it was still murky. 'Saddle up all of you. Sam, do the best you can to make Jase comfortable. He'll just have to share with any calves that are born.'

So that was it. Peck had come out on top, for all to see. As Ewing made for his horse, he realized that there was far more to a cattle drive than merely surviving it!

*

Three more days of relatively uneventful travel saw the Bar E herd approaching the south bank of the Colorado River. They had been averaging fifteen miles each day, which was about as good as it got on a cattle drive. There were many more rivers to come, and it was a fact that crossing them would be akin to climbing the rungs of a ladder heading north. After long hours and little sleep, the environs of San Antonio felt like a distant memory.

Sadly, not *everything* was hunky dory. Although splinted efficiently, Jase Spooner's leg was showing no signs of improving. In fact it seemed to be getting a whole lot worse. As John Ewing sat on his horse, contemplating the watercourse, Sam wheeled his wagon over to within twenty-five yards. The teamster then brought it to a halt, climbed down and walked the rest of the way. That in itself was unusual, because few trail hands walked anywhere if they could help it. And, possibly because he didn't make his living from the back of a horse, he was the tallest man on the drive and powerfully built with it.

'What I got to say is best not overheard by a certain party,' he remarked. His face was entirely devoid of warmth. Only when the trail boss had dismounted did he continue. 'His leg is starting to smell bad. You know what that means, don't you?'

Ewing pushed his plains hat back on his head and sighed. 'Oh shit! His leg is gonna have to come off, ain't it?'

Sam nodded glumly. 'Reckon it's the only way I know of to stop greenrod spreading. Then again, the doing of it will likely kill him anyhu, so I guess it's got to be your call, boss.'

Ewing nodded his understanding. This was to be the first decision of any importance that had been required of him since his set to with Peck, but this time it required very little thought. 'In camp tonight, after we've crossed the river.' He took a deep breath and grimaced. 'I'll do the cutting.'

Sam's eyebrows rose. 'You right sure about that, boss? Only you won't know it, but I've had cause to do such once before.'

Ewing shook his head, perhaps a little too emphatically. 'It's right that I do it. I brought him out here, so it's my responsibility. But I'd be obliged if you'd guide me through it, and maybe employ your strength to hold him down. The sheep dip that passes for whiskey ain't likely to handle his pain.' He paused for a moment, as something occurred to him. 'The time before. Did he make it?'

The teamster's strong features were suddenly tinged with sadness. 'Died before my very eyes, the poor bastard!'

CHAPTER FOUR

This crossing had mercifully occurred without incident, and now the entire herd was north of the Colorado River. With nightfall approaching, Ewing ordered a welcome halt. Plenty of lush grazing meant they had reached as good a place as any to make camp. And the fresh water at their backs acted as a natural barrier. That way, if the dumb animals should decide to stampede, they would have fewer options available. Even when well fed, it took very little to make them skittish.

With the evening's chow consumed and the utensils washed clean, there would normally have been a soulful tune from 'Mesquite' Bill's harmonica, or maybe some tall tales. But not that night. An air of expectation hung over the tired hands. Somehow, word had gone round, and it seemed as though everyone knew what was about to happen . . . except the patient. And it was then that Vernon Peck chose to offer his own contribution. As though deliberately

42

courting an audience, he made no attempt at discretion.

'Wouldn't it make more sense to do this during the day?' he queried across the flickering light of one of the campfires.

'No, it wouldn't!' Ewing snapped back. With Sam's bone saw warming over the fire, he was already uncomfortably on edge. The big teamster was in the back of his wagon, gently easing whiskey down their unsuspecting patient's throat.

Peck merely shrugged before trying again. 'Only, he gets to screaming, an' it could spook the herd. In daylight you could drop back, an' then catch up once the deed is done.'

John Ewing knew full well that he and his old comrade were now the full focus of attention in the camp, and he could feel raw anger building within him. What the hell was Vern trying to do, deliberately create a rift between them?

'No!' he barked out, rather more loudly than he had intended. 'This way he gets time to rest for the night before we're on the move again. He deserves every chance we . . . *I* can give him.'

Peck submissively held his hands out. 'OK, OK. You're the boss. Just having my say, is all.'

'Yes, I am,' Ewing frostily remarked. 'And it would do well for everyone to remember that fact!' Before anyone could comment, he turned to a group of his men loafing near a fire. 'You fellas, lift Jase out of the wagon and lay him over here. Gently now.'

Those last two words, uttered in the heat of the

moment, drew reproachful glances from the drovers who had only Spooner's best interests at heart, but nevertheless they complied in silence. All of the hands seemed to have recognized that something wasn't quite right between the two older men. It was as though Peck was deliberately needling the trail boss.

Four men took hold of the blanket on the wagon bed, and with Sam supporting Spooner's head they carried him over to where Ewing waited nervously. The young man twitched and groaned, but appeared blissfully unaware of just what was in store. Having eased him to the ground, his friends stood around uncomfortably staring at the doomed lower leg. When the bone had fractured, the two ends had moved out of line puncturing the skin. Even though splinted into position, infection had taken hold. The torn flesh was now discoloured and becoming increasingly foul smelling.

Ewing stared long and hard at the man he was about to butcher. Then, kneeling down next to him, he glanced over at Sam. 'You got something to put between his teeth?'

'I reckon this will answer,' that man replied as he produced a leather boot sole, and gently inserted it between Spooner's teeth. He had obviously assumed the role of surgeon's assistant, for which his boss was extremely grateful.

'So let's get it done.' Gesturing at the bone saw, Ewing added, 'Where the hell did you get this thing, anyhu?'

Sam favoured him with a half smile. 'I stole it from an ornery sawbones in Creede, Colorado! Never can tell when I might need to lop a limb off.'

In addition to the purloined saw, the reluctant practitioner possessed a skinning knife and a small pot of coal tar for sealing the wound. He watched as Sam arranged himself across Spooner's chest, and readied a jug of whiskey. With two drovers having seized an ankle each, it really was time for the primitive surgery to begin.

Ewing sucked in a steadying breath, lined the knife up on a section of flesh just above his patient's left knee, and nodded. Sam poured the liquid over the blade, and then watched as the well-honed edge suddenly cut deep. No whiskey-induced stupor could handle the resultant pain, and Spooner emitted a tremendous muffled groan whilst trying to arch his back. Sam's weight effectively prevented that, and the drovers kept both legs pinioned to the blanket.

All of the Bar E employees, with the exception of the two 'night hawks', were glued to the unfolding nightmare. With sweat pouring from him, John Ewing sliced around the thigh in a circular motion until the bone was fully visible. His breath was coming in short, sharp gasps, and his heart was thumping like an anvil strike. Not even in the war had he been called upon to perform anything like this. And yet it was nothing compared to what his patient had to be suffering. Dropping the knife as though it was white hot, he next took hold of the saw. Speed was paramount, or Spooner would surely die of blood loss.

Shifting position slightly, Sam unknowingly eased his pressure on the leather pad just as the saw bit into bone. The agonised drover screamed out his torment into the night, and the result was almost immediate. Those steers nearest the camp began to stir nervously. Ewing had too much on his mind to consider the consequences, but Sam recognized the danger. Desperately, he tried to force the pad back between Spooner's teeth, but not before he had unleashed another unearthly wail. That was just too much for the nearby cattle. Thoroughly spooked, they began to shove into their neighbours, which in turn unsettled them. Then, before the 'night hawks' horrified gaze, the whole herd was suddenly on the move.

Almost with relief, Reno tore his eyes from the horrific scene by the fire and shouted, 'Mount up boys. We got us a stampede!'

Although dimly perceiving the sudden frantic activity around him, the trail boss had far more immediate problems of his own. The thighbone is the thickest in the human body, and he had never cut through anything like it before. Now literally drenched in both sweat and his patient's blood, he sawed away like a maniac. Sam and the two remaining drovers could only hold on tight and watch his desperate efforts. And then, quite abruptly, Jase Spooner simply stopped struggling.

For a moment, the teamster thought the young man had passed out, until he realized that his breathing had ceased. Totally oblivious, Ewing continued running the serrated saw back and forth across the glistening bone.

'He's gone, boss,' Sam announced, but still the amateur 'sawbones' maintained his frenetic motion. 'For Christ sake, man, he's dead!'

Only then did Ewing raise his head and stare fixedly at his employee. His eyes were those of a man possessed, but at least he finally stopped sawing. Then, as he allowed the bloodied implement to fall from his clawed hand, he gasped, 'What's happened?'

'He just up and stopped breathing, boss,' Sam softly explained. 'Shock, blood loss, who the hell knows. Maybe his heart gave out. You did your best, is all.'

As though for the first time, Ewing glanced down at the tortured figure and despairingly shook his head. Guilt overwhelmed him, as he realized that if he'd released enough men for escort duty to San Antonio this could have been avoided. Temporarily exhausted, had he been standing he would undoubtedly have collapsed. Then, slowly, events out there in the darkness began to register. Peering around, he realized that the camp was deserted. Even the cook was missing. And, more to the point, so were his cattle.

'Oh shit!' he exclaimed. 'The herd.'

The speed at which he was travelling through the gloom was pure lunacy, but Reno had no other thought than to get ahead of the runaway steers. He could sense other riders around him, but risking a quick glance, he was mighty surprised to find that one of them was the gunhand. He hadn't realized that Peck was such a competent horseman.

'We need to get up to the leaders,' the top hand bellowed out.

It was a fact that the best way to end a stampede was to turn those at the front, and then *keep* turning them in ever decreasing circles until their own numbers brought them to a halt.

The exhilaration and excitement of riding through the night at high speed effectively masked the very real danger . . . until it up and bit someone. A drover going by the name of Jim Stimson was eager to prove his worth by reaching point first. Urging his mount to greater efforts, he had no way of spotting the lurking gopher hole. Without warning, the poor horse lurched forward, breaking a leg and throwing its rider. Stimson hit the ground with bruising force that left him winded and helpless. Left to his own devices, he would no doubt have recovered, but his proximity to the charging herd meant that instead he and his horse were promptly trampled to a bloody pulp by countless hoofs. Such was the pace of events that his gruesome demise barely registered with the others as they swept past.

It was Reno who finally got ahead of the front-runners. Unsheathing his old Henry Rifle, he single-handedly levered in a cartridge and fired into the air. Then, as the lead steers nervously edged away from him, he urged his horse to the right. Following his example, Peck drew a revolver and also opened fire at the night sky. Their concerted efforts soon began to pay off. Although the herd showed no sign of slowing, it did begin to turn on itself.

Keen to be able to relate that he had played a major part, a drover called Josiah Griswold eagerly began to crowd the animals next to him. He was acting recklessly and should have known better, because they weren't called *Longhorns* for nothing. One of them jerked its head to the left, and casually impaled the belly of his horse. Literally screaming in agony, the pitiful creature slewed sideways, depositing its rider in the midst of the charging herd. His became the second brutal death in as many minutes.

Up ahead, the continued gunfire and careful manoeuvring had the cattle running in the makings of a wide circle that would have only one ultimate result. And sure enough, as the leading steers closed the loop, they found themselves confronted by others of their ilk. All they could do was continue to turn, and inevitably their momentum slowed. The mad rush was burning itself out, but its consequences would be far reaching.

John Ewing had been torn by indecision. His instinctive urge was to follow the herd, but hard logic decreed that since it was already so far distant he stood no chance of influencing the outcome of the stampede. Far better instead to help Sam with the desperately sad task of digging a grave, so that when

Spooner's buddies eventually returned they wouldn't be faced with his dismembered corpse.

As it turned out, only half a dozen riders ultimately reappeared, because there was little point in driving the cattle south after the dumb creatures had at least had the decency to stampede *towards* Abilene. It made much more sense to move camp to where the animals had finally run out of steam. One of the men, Nico Montoya, dismounted shakily and headed straight for the familiar security of his chuck wagon. Assisting the drovers had initially seemed preferable to witnessing an amputation, but now he wasn't so sure. The others, who of course just had to include Vernon Peck, sat their horses and contemplated the freshly covered grave. It was Mesquite Bill who had the words. A normally respectful employee, he now glanced scathingly at his boss.

'Better get to digging some more of those,' he rasped.

Ewing stared at him in shocked disbelief, but before he could respond, the drover added, 'You know how many dead we got?'

A dreadful chill enveloped the trail boss. It appeared as though the night was going from bad to worse. And yet nevertheless, despite everything that had happened, he didn't care for the other man's insubordinate tone. 'Well obviously I don't, but I think you'd better tell me,' he remarked frostily.

'Stimson and Griswold ain't got a bone left to break in their bodies,' Bill replied bitterly. 'In fact we had all on recognizing them. An' all 'cause you wouldn't listen to Vern's counsel.'

'Oh, so it's *Vern* now, is it?' Ewing retorted mockingly. Then he glimpsed Spooner's grave, and he realized that he had to get a grip on the situation. 'Look men, I know we're all hurting, but what's done is done.' While speaking, he glanced at his old *compadre.* Peck's eyes momentarily locked with his before narrowing slightly and shifting away. It was at that instant that Ewing realized something was going on that just didn't sit right. The problem was, he didn't know what . . . yet. One thing did need addressing though.

'The passing of these three men is a terrible waste, and believe me I feel it as badly as you. I made the call, and I've got to live with it. But it's no one's fault . . . unless you blame snakes and longhorns. And it sure doesn't change anything. Because come what may, we're taking the Bar E cattle to Kansas, and until we get there you all answer to me. Understood?'

As though suddenly coming to terms with reality, embarrassment replaced belligerence on Bill's features. 'Yeah boss. Sure thing, and . . . sorry. I guess the state of them shook me up, is all.'

Ewing silently looked all five men over before acknowledging the apology. And he had more to say about the victims of the stampede. 'It's a pure shame about Griswold and Stimson. They were good men both. If anyone's got a Bible, I'll read over them once we make camp again. Now get all this gear loaded into Sam's wagon.'

As the men dismounted and hurried to do his

51

bidding, Ewing called out, 'Vern, get yourself over here.'

As that man ambled over to join him, there was no sign of any animosity on his features, but that didn't cut any ice with the weary trail boss. 'Just what the hell are you about, Vern? Ever since you joined this drive you've been sniping at me.'

Peck's lean face registered apparent surprise. 'Seems to me like you're jumping at shadows, old friend,' he replied easily. 'Just been having my say, is all. You wouldn't expect any less, would you?'

Ewing frowned. 'What I expect is for you to back me up when I make a decision . . . even if you don't agree with it. Because that's what friends are for. That and the fact I'm paying your wages!'

A broad smile suddenly appeared on Peck's face. 'Well sure, John. Shit, I didn't mean nothing by it. I guess it's just my contrary nature, is all.' With that he stuck out his right hand. 'No hard feelings, huh?'

Ewing instinctively accepted the firm grip, and began to wonder whether he'd overreacted. After all, he was tired and badly shaken by the death of three men. The manner of Spooner's demise in particular had really got under his skin. Quite literally in fact, because the poor man's blood was still under his fingernails. And yet, even as they parted, there was still a niggle in the back of his mind . . . because one thing he had never done was jump at shadows. It didn't occur to him that there could always be a first time!

*

The following morning, it transpired that Nico Montoya was the only man in the relocated camp who possessed a Bible, which he willingly loaned to his employer. The simple service, with all the men standing bareheaded around the two graves, was soon over, because as ever they were burning daylight. And as John Ewing perhaps over-optimistically remarked, 'This is the last time on this drive that we'll still be in camp come daybreak.'

For the next three days the Bar E cattle continued their journey north without further incident. The hands had fatalistically accepted the loss of their *compadres*, and even Vernon Peck had uncharacteristically maintained a low profile. The next river of significance, and one that was shortly to be encountered, was the Brazos. After that it would be the Red River on Texas's northern border, which would see them into the land designated by the US Government as Indian Territory.

Late in the afternoon, John Ewing was sweeping down the left flank, on his way to check out a suitable river crossing for the following morning, when Sam caught his attention. Slowing down next to the teamster, he noted that there were now four newly born calves on the wagon bed. Such additions to the herd surely justified the presence of another vehicle, but the individual in charge of it was about to prove his worth in other ways.

'Controlling these ornery mules don't take up all of my time,' he remarked obliquely from under his plains hat. 'I get time to look around this fine country as well.'

Ewing wasn't really in the mood for riddles, but he recognized the big man's serious demeanour and so chose to humour him. 'And what would I see if I was to do the same?'

'Well if you was to have eyes akin to a hawk, you'd like as not catch sight of a line of riders paralleling the herd. Off to our left, well back in the trees. I only saw them at all because sunlight flashed on some metalwork.'

Despite the sun's warmth, Ewing felt a chill spread over his body. 'Indians?'

Sam emphatically shook his head. 'Nah. Not unless them poxy dirt worshippers have taken to wearing plains hats and duster coats.'

The trail boss's mind was suddenly like a seething maelstrom. It took a supreme effort of will not to turn and stare hard at those same trees. 'How long have they been shadowing us?'

Sam shrugged. 'Spotted them about an hour ago, but that don't mean shit. They could have been out there for days. Maybe even back as far as San Antonio. What counts is that they don't want us to see them.'

John Ewing bleakly viewed the other man. 'Which can only mean one thing. Unlike the Comanches, who only wanted a few steers, this outfit is surely after the whole herd!'

CHAPTER FIVE

For the rest of that day, and most of the following night, John Ewing had agonised over what course of action to take. Having surreptitiously placed a draw-tube spyglass across his saddle, he had confirmed beyond any doubt the existence of the distant group. And one thing was for sure, the men out there, whoever they were, could only have hostile intentions.

Jerking awake after barely two hours sleep, he lay on his bedroll in the pre-dawn darkness and soon everything became so clear. Whoever those men were out there, he could not allow them the first move. He would get the herd safely across the Brazos, and then come nightfall take some volunteers and go looking for trouble.

Movement registered nearby, and Ewing glanced over to watch Montoya preparing breakfast for the hands. Morbidly, he wondered if their numbers would be reduced even more come the next dawn. The thought of yet more men dying in his employ tormented him something terrible. With a groan, he rolled off the blanket and staggered to his feet. Such thoughts did no one any good, and in any case it was time to be up and about.

As the hired men assembled for the ubiquitous beans and coffee, their boss came to a decision. Better to tell them everything than to let the news of the latest threat drift out piecemeal. And so, as his men ate their fill, Ewing explained his predicament and asked for volunteers. 'I aim to catch them in the dark, unawares, but no one can foretell how such things will turn out. There could be some killing, so I won't be ill disposed to any man that doesn't want to come. And I only need maybe half a dozen or so. That's enough of us to be stumbling around in the dark.'

Almost inevitably it was Peck who was the first to speak up. 'An' if you do happen to catch them unawares, then what?'

Ewing was ready for such a question, and so replied without hesitation. 'We will take all their weapons and send them on their way. If they should be unlucky enough to encounter any savages after that, well . . . that'll be their problem.'

Peck favoured him with a lop-sided smile. 'Seems like you got it all thought out, *boss*. So I reckon I'd better be your first volunteer. You might could have need of these Colts.'

Ewing's return smile was unforced and genuine. 'I might at that, and thank you kindly, Vern.'

Other men, encouraged by the 'gunhand's' enthusiasm, quickly put their hands up, and Ewing soon

had far more than he required. And so, feeling temporarily lighter in spirit than he had for some time,
the trail boss made the inevitable announcement.
'Mount up. We're burning daylight!'

Sadly, John Ewing's buoyant mood only lasted until
mid-morning. The vanguard of the herd arrived at
the Brazos and began to cross at the place he had
identified the previous afternoon. All went well, and
under the urging of the drovers the cattle safely
splashed across to the far side. Nico Montoya,
knowing how risky river crossings could be, held his
chuck wagon back until he had the watercourse to
himself. Of course, the depth was already known, but
the consistency of the riverbed less so, and therefore
he took it very carefully.

Stopping briefly to allow his mules to drink, the
cook nervously searched the flow for any signs of
snakes. Then, with pans and utensils rattling away,
the heavily laden wagon continued safely across to
the north bank. Dripping water, the front wheels
emerged onto the slope. Montoya urged his team to
greater speed, and up they went until the front of the
vehicle was on level ground. So far so good.

The rear wheels supported the greatest weight,
and it was as they went up the bank that, without any
warning, a section of it collapsed directly beneath the
right-hand one. With a tremendous crack, two of its
wooden spokes shattered, allowing the outer rim to
buckle. Montoya felt the sudden drag, and had the
presence of mind to whip his team of four into

greater efforts. The cook's quick thinking worked . . . but only just. When the back of the chuck wagon joined him on flat, dry land, it was immediately obvious that it wouldn't be travelling any further. Not with the wheel as it was, anyway.

'Goddamn it all to hell!' John Ewing exclaimed when he saw the damage. 'We really didn't need this.'

'I'm sorry, Mister Ewing,' Montoya replied with genuine remorse. 'The riverbank, it just fell away.'

'Yeah, yeah, I know. Bad things happen. Just seems like we've had more than our far share, is all. Anyhu, you'll have to fix it and catch us up.'

The cook was aghast. 'All alone? Is not possible!'

Despite the situation, the trail boss had to laugh. 'Nah, I'm not that much of a hard nose.' Turning to Peck, who was still riding drag, he hollered for him to collect Sam and drop back to join them.

A short while later, the other wagon arrived and the teamster speculatively viewed the damage.

'Can you and Nico fix this by yourselves?' Ewing demanded. 'Only I'm a mite shorthanded.'

The big teamster nodded slowly. 'It'll take us a while, but yeah, it can be done. I've got some spare spokes and tools in the back of my wagon. We'll just have to unload some of his stuff to lighten it.'

Ewing made his decision. 'Right. Get what you need. We'll help with the shifting before we leave. Vern, you take over Sam's wagon until he catches us up. We can't separate the calves from the herd for too long. And get enough chow out of the chuck wagon to last us the night. Just in case.'

Shortly after, with Montoya's wagon partially emptied, Vern and Ewing set off after the herd. 'You be sure an' look after my mules, damn it!' Sam hollered.

Peck waved casually without even turning, whereas the trail boss reined in for a moment to glance back at the two men and their crippled conveyance. Alone in the vast expanse of the Southern Plains, to his eyes they suddenly appeared very vulnerable indeed, but there could be no help for it. The herd had to be kept moving, and being three men short, he couldn't spare any drovers to stay with them, especially with what he had planned for nightfall. And whoever was shadowing them, was likely just interested in the herd. Wandering bands of Comanches and Kiowas were the biggest threat to Sam and Nico, but they would just have to take their chances. With that bleak assessment, Ewing turned and urged his mount into motion.

As the sun fell over the western horizon, the herd was brought to a halt and the hands collected the makings for the usual fires. Everything was to occur as normal, so that anyone observing them through a spyglass would get no hint of what was intended. Ewing had already decided on who was to accompany him. Naturally Peck was to be one of the group. The other four were men who maintained that they were reasonable hands with a six-gun. Reno had nervously volunteered and been refused. If anything befell the trail boss, he wanted a top man available to control the herd on the considerable journey still remaining. And besides, Reno appeared far too affable to stand against a gang of possible gun thugs.

The trail boss felt pangs of anxiety as the last of the light drained out of the sky. The chuck wagon still hadn't reappeared, but he couldn't allow that to alter his plans. They had food enough to last them until the next day, and all of the hands now had their sidearms strapped to their waists. The prohibition against wearing them was one rule that sadly hadn't survived long on the drive.

'Once you've eaten,' he instructed. 'I want every man to check his weapons . . . but not so as anyone might see from off to my left.'

Campfires were doubling as cooking fires, but even though the aromas were tempting, those due to leave camp shortly had to force their food down . . . with the sole exception of Peck, who appeared to genuinely relish his bacon and beans. And then, after what seemed like an interminable wait filled by desultory conversation, it was time. The six men casually drifted out of the firelight, as though they were heading for their bedrolls. In reality, they made for their horses, which had been deliberately tethered well clear of any fires.

As they mounted up, Peck gave his first and only piece of advice. 'If it comes to shooting, aim to kill, 'cause we'll likely be outnumbered. Savvy?'

Two of the drovers swallowed nervously. It's a hell of a thing to take a man's life, and probably only Peck and Ewing had done so. Slowly walking their mounts out of camp, the small raiding party maintained that pace as they rode west. It behoved them to make as little noise as possible, at the start of what, for them, was likely to be a long and possibly dangerous night.

Once away from the firelight, their eyes soon became accustomed to the dark. They were making for a large stand of oak trees that had been visible before nightfall, approximately two miles from the herd. This seemed to be the logical place for anyone following them to make camp. For those outlawed up and with bad intentions, it would also have made sense to embrace a cold camp, but as it turned out this particular group was overly confident of their having remained unseen.

After nearly one hour of walking their animals, the six men spotted flickering light in the trees ahead. 'Stupid bastards!' Peck muttered under his breath.

Ewing immediately reined in, dismounted, and produced a picket pin from his pocket. He was promptly copied by the others. 'Ground tether the horses here,' he whispered. 'We're far enough away for any whinnying not to be heard. Then spread out, but keep me in sight as you follow on.'

It came to mind, as he waited for them to comply, that it was like being back in the war, approaching a Yankee encampment. Those sons of bitches had always been well endowed with supplies, and often careless. A slight sheen of sweat suddenly coated his brow, as unwelcome memories flooded back. Undoubtedly, this sort of action was food and drink

61

for Vernon Peck, but not so for him. In fact it was something he had prayed would never occur again.

Glancing from left to right, Ewing could just make out the most distant of his shadowy companions. With cloud obscuring the moon, the darkness was working in their favour for once. Tightly clutching his Colt Army, he began a steady advance on the unknown party. As they got nearer, snippets of conversation could be heard through the trees, and it was pretty obvious that the men were sharing a jug of whiskey.

'I'm sick of this pussyfooting around,' came a loud voice. 'We ought to just ride on in there and take them steers!' The words were slurred, so that 'steers' came out as 'shhteers'.

'Hah, that's rich,' retorted another. 'You couldn't tell a steer from a pronghorn if they was to shit on your boots!'

That drew chuckles from the group, and more particularly a grim smile from John Ewing. The rustlers were quite obviously completely unaware of his presence, and their talk had definitely confirmed Sam's assumptions. Whatever happened next would therefore be entirely legal.

Now inside the tree line, he stopped to check the positions of his men. Peck was just behind him and to the right, clutching both Colt Navys. His capable figure provided reassurance to the trail boss and the others, because it was now pretty obvious that they were outnumbered. From what Ewing could make out in the flickering light, there were approximately a dozen men lounging around the fire. Feeling sure that the thumping from his heart must give them all away, he decided that it was time to make his move. There was what seemed to be a deafening double click as he cocked his revolver.

'Don't any of you pus weasels reach for a gun,' he barked out. 'Or it will surely go badly for you!'

About the fire there was a stunned silence, as every man present twisted around towards the oak trees. Then the five Bar E hands cocked their weapons, leaving the potential rustlers in no doubt that their night time callers had very deadly intentions. Emboldened by the lack of response, Ewing continued.

'Now, I want every mother's son of you to lie on your backs and unbuckle your gunbelts. Be sure and keep your hands well clear of those shooting irons.'

'I don't know who the hell you are, mister,' whined one of the outlaws. 'But you got no call to be treating us like this. We ain't just common felons!'

'I just heard you talking about my herd,' Ewing retorted. 'You're outlawed up, for sure. So do as I said, or get to dying!'

Vernon Peck glanced at the drovers on either side of him. All of their attention was focused on the men around the fire. A chill smile appeared on his features as he levelled his Navy Sixes at the two Bar E men furthest away on each side. Although both presented narrow targets, they were motionless and completely unsuspecting. He triggered his right-hand Colt first, which discharged with a satisfying crash. Without even checking on the result, Peck swivelled his head to the left and fired his other revolver. That too flashed in the night, and this time he saw his victim jerk to one side and collapse.

The unexpected gunfire caused pandemonium among both groups. Those by the fire assumed that Ewing had come good on his threat, whilst he and his surviving men thought that one of their own had defensively opened fire . . . which in a perverse way was true. As some of the outlaws instinctively reached for their guns, the trail boss cursed under his breath. He really hadn't wanted it to come to this, but since it had he would make them pay dearly. Ducking behind a tree, he swiftly drew a bead on the nearest man and fired.

The Colt Army in his right hand, chambered for a .44 calibre lead ball, was intended as a man stopper. Ewing's first shot struck his victim in the chest. That man coughed up blood and fell back on his bedroll. With practised speed, Ewing cocked and fired again at someone who had leapt to his feet and was aiming at him. This time he struck his prey just above the upper lip. The heavy ball flattened out inside his skull and exploded through the back of his head in a shower of bone fragments and fluids. The outlaw was dead before he hit the ground.

Still not even realizing that their companions were deceased, the two remaining drovers also opened fire in support of their boss, but they were less skilled and deliberate than he. One ball struck a leather boot, blowing off a big toe inside it, whilst the other merely slammed into a log on the fire. Still hanging back, Peck again cocked both revolvers and simultaneously took aim at the two men. With the skill of a true 'pistolero', he managed to drop them both without either of them realizing who had done it.

John Ewing heard lead smacking into the tree before him, but he suddenly had more pressing concerns. Glancing around in the gloom, it dawned on him that he appeared to have no men left standing. Turning, he dimly perceived a single figure. His night vision had been spoiled by the fire, but there could be no mistaking the two Colts pointing at him.

'Vern, what the hell are you about?' he demanded.

The answer was one he could never have expected. With a muzzle flash flaring out before him, a hammer blow seemed to strike his left shoulder, and Ewing fell back against the tree. As his body convulsed with shock, the Colt Army fell from his grip. Even through the terrible pain, he tried to comprehend what had just happened.

'You just stay where you are, John, or I'll surely put another piece of lead in you,' Peck commanded softly. Then a wildly aimed ball struck a nearby tree and he bellowed out, 'Stop that shooting, you miserable cockchafers! There ain't no one left back here toting any firearms but me, Vernon Peck.'

For a moment there was silence. Then a befuddled voice called out, 'Vern? Is that you?'

'I just said so, didn't I? You useless bastard!' Peck snarled back.

'Hot dang,' another cried out. 'It really is him.

65

Where'd you spring from?'

Rather than answer, Peck slowly walked over to Ewing's trembling figure. After peering at him closely for a moment, he bent down and retrieved the Colt Army, but for some obscure reason left him his sheath knife. Then, nodding with satisfaction, he tucked the revolver in his belt, turned away and approached the camp. Of the twelve gun thugs occupying it, two were now dead, while a third moaned in agony as he struggled to remove his blood-soaked boot.

As he stared at the survivors, Peck's features registered utter contempt. 'You bull turds really ain't worth a damn. You just couldn't do as you were told and stay out of sight, could you? If I hadn't come along with these fellas, you'd all be trussed up like Thanksgiving turkeys about now. As it is, them drovers over yonder are gonna be even more short-handed when they come to move that herd next. Which means you'll have to help them.'

'Aw hell, Vern,' whined one of the rustlers. 'How was we to know they'd done spotted us?'

Peck just sighed and holstered one of his Navy Sixes. Turning back towards John Ewing, he levelled the other revolver. Staring at the gaping muzzle, Ewing gritted his teeth but remained silent. He wasn't about to provide satisfaction by pleading for his life. The gunhand gazed long and hard at him, his forefinger tightening on the trigger. Then, taking into account the bloodied shoulder and ashen features, he finally grunted and shook his head. 'For old

66

time's sake I've agreed with myself that I'll let you live,' he stated flatly. 'But if you try to follow us, I *will* finish the job.'

'Kill him, Vern. Kill him,' sputtered one of the rustlers. 'He done kilt two of us for no good reason.'

'Shut your tarnal mouth, Stiles!' Peck barked. 'Or I'll kick you so hard, you'll be wearing your ass for a hat!' Then he issued a concise series of orders that confirmed beyond any doubt just who was in charge. 'Make sure none of these drovers are still breathing, and collect up their shooting irons. Any coins in their pockets belong to me, seeing as how it was me what kilt them. And there's five horses back there that are going with us. Smash that keg of whiskey against a rock, an' get all the vittles together. Ewing's chuck wagon bust a wheel back down the trail a ways, so they ain't flush with food. An' for Christ sake, someone bandage Breck's foot. All his bleating is making my head hurt. Then we're moving out.'

With his blood-soaked shoulder throbbing like the devil, Ewing watched as the men went about their tasks. It was only as they all mounted up to depart that he finally spoke. 'What happened to you, Vern? You used to be someone I could trust . . . just about.'

Peck glanced calmly over at him. His response was entirely unrepentant. 'You're still alive, ain't you?'

CHAPTER SIX

'Jesus, Reno,' Buckskin Joe exclaimed. 'That sure was an awful lot of shooting. Don't you think we should go take a look see?'

The top hand frowned unhappily. He knew all there was to know about tending animals, but tackling rustlers was something else again. For long moments he peered hopefully towards the distant mass of trees. In truth, he couldn't see a damn thing, and was in no all fired hurry to go looking.

'Nah. I reckon we should just stay put,' he managed eventually. 'Mister Ewing didn't say nothing about watching over him.'

And so, for what seemed like an age, the cowhands remained in camp, nervously waiting on whoever turned up. All of them, including the two nighthawks, had their holster guns drawn. If Reno had possessed more experience of such matters, he would have doused the fires. As it was, with their night vision compromised, the voice from the gloom took them completely by surprise.

'Hello the camp. It's me, Peck. I'm coming in. Don't go popping any caps on me, you hear?'

Only then did a horseman slowly materialise out of the darkness. As it became obvious that he was alone, relief turned to concern.

'Where the hell are the others? Where's the boss?' Reno demanded.

Peck tethered his horse to a picket line, and made straight for the nearest coffee pot. 'Been me, I'd have doused this lot. You're all just targets, sat like dummies around these fires.'

Reno blinked, as recognition of their vulnerability hit him. 'OK, OK. But where are they, for Christ sake?'

Peck sighed, but calmly drank some coffee before answering. 'Well I'll tell you, boys. It was a dark result. There were some killings, an' John took a ball in his shoulder. The others are tending to him as best they can, an' hog tying them varmints we didn't shoot.' He paused to view the ripple of shock that had swept over the camp. 'Thing is,' the gunhand continued smoothly, 'He's kind of worried about gunfire spooking the herd. So seeing as how them rustlers have been dealt with, he wants you to stash your gunbelts in Sam's wagon. Sent me on ahead to tell you.'

Reno stared at him incredulously. 'You got to be joshing me!'

As before his fight with the Comanches, the flesh tightened across Peck's cheekbones. 'Do I look like I am?'

The drover's mouth opened, but no words came. Then he glanced around at the others. Some of them shrugged, whilst others looked away, but none of them chose to argue. Although not a man there would care to admit it, all of them were intimidated by Vernon Peck. An air of menace seemed to hang over him, and most of them had seen the dead Comanches after he had finished with them.

Finally, rather than answer him directly, Reno simply unbuckled his gunbelt. 'Best do as he says, boys.'

Mesquite Bill's was the only dissenting voice. 'Well it seems like pure foolishness to me. What if there's more of them thieving sons of bitches out yonder that we don't know about?'

Reno's hackles began to rise. Secretly he agreed, but hadn't the grit to challenge Peck. 'Goddamn it all, Bill. Just do it. Mister Ewing's got enough on his plate without us acting up.'

And so, very reluctantly, all the hands disarmed themselves, with Peck as the sole exception. It was only a few short minutes after the last gunbelt had been grudgingly placed in the wagon that they all heard the sound of approaching hoof beats. The moaning of a man in pain was also audible, which could only mean one thing. All turned to catch sight of their wounded employer.

The ten riders who came into view in a wide semi-circle were complete strangers, and all except one had a gun pointing at the startled drovers. The injured man obviously had other things on his mind,

70

but noticeably not from any damage to his shoulder.

With surprise affecting his comprehension, Bill barked out, 'What the hell is all this?'

Behind him, Peck chuckled. 'From where I'm standing, I'd say you've all just been suckered.'

Reno was flabbergasted. 'But all that shooting! You said that. . . .'

Peck shook his head dismissively, as though he was now becoming bored with the whole business. 'I lied. OK? And to get my hands on all this cash on the hoof, I'd do it agin.' Glancing around at the assembled drovers, he added, 'An' you're lucky we need you all to drive the herd, 'cause otherwise you'd be paroled to Jesus like your *compadres* over yonder.' A thought suddenly occurred to him. 'Reno. Get the night hawks back in here, pronto. I want their guns off of them as well. Oh, and while you're about it, every man's long gun goes into the back of the wagon, too. From now on, the only *hombres* who go heeled in this outfit are me and mine.'

The top hand seemed to be in the middle of a bad dream, but he soon proved that his wits were returning, albeit far too late. 'And what if I don't. You can't shoot me for fear of stampeding the herd.'

The gunhand sighed impatiently . . . and immediately produced a knife from a sheath on his belt. 'Don't test my patience, boy! Or I'll get to whittling on you with this cutting tool. With a kerchief stuffed in your mouth, them steers won't hear a thing!'

As Reno took in both the honed blade and his

71

opponent's gritted teeth, he swallowed uncomfortably and peered around for support. That none was forthcoming came as no surprise to anyone. All recognized Peck's lethal abilities. His cronies sniggered as the young drover's shoulders slumped in defeat. The herd was theirs, only rather sooner than they had expected!

For a long while after the rustlers disappeared into the darkness, John Ewing sat with his back to the oak tree. It wasn't that he didn't want to get up. He simply couldn't. His shoulder throbbed abominably and he felt light-headed. Then he began to dwell on Peck's role in the whole bloody business, and raw anger coursed through his veins. It was almost beyond comprehension that the man who had saved his life in the war had deliberately plotted to steal his cattle. Yet that was exactly what was happening. And then there were the killings. Within as many yards of him, four of his drovers lay dead. His men and his responsibility!

With a supreme effort, and using the tree as leverage, Ewing staggered to his feet. For a few desperately unpleasant moments his head seemed to spin uncontrollably, and he felt sure that he must fall. Then, gradually, his balance returned. Instinctively, his hand dropped to his holster. Empty. 'Goddamn it all to hell!' he muttered.

Tentatively attempting a first step, he swayed and fell back against the same tree, but managed to remain upright. Consciously drawing in deep breaths, he next reached up to examine the shoulder wound. That there was an entry hole was undoubted. The question was, had the ball continued right through.

With the effort causing sweat to suddenly pour from him, the trail boss ran the fingers of his right hand around the back. Sure enough, there was also an exit wound. The lead appeared to have missed bone, and instead gone through the meaty flesh below the shoulder joint, before disappearing into the night. So far, so good, *but* . . . had any piece of clothing been taken into the wound? Because if it had, then infection might set in, guaranteeing a certain and unpleasant death.

Shuffling over to the remnants of the fire, he dropped to his knees with a groan. Ignoring the pain, Ewing carefully inspected his torn shirt for any missing fabric. Although a hole had been punched through the cotton, it didn't appear that any was missing. Sighing with relief, he suddenly spotted the remnants of the whiskey keg. Although smashed against a rock, the bottom section was upright. Crawling over to it, he grunted with satisfaction. A decent shot of the raw spirit remained.

Flouting his own rule against any drinking on the drive, the injured man first took a sip of it. 'Christ, what did they put in this?' he gasped. Then he ripped away more of the material and lay down next to the fire. Steeling himself against the inevitable agony, he poured the 'who hit John' over his torn and bloody flesh. The shock was such that he howled out into the night like a timber wolf.

For long moments, Ewing lay panting on the hard ground. He had no inclination to move, but then the recollection of Vernon Peck's Colt Navy prompted him into stirring. What if the bastard decided that it had been a big mistake to let him live? At all costs, he needed to put some distance between himself and this killing ground before daybreak.

A strong desire to survive provided the now redundant trail boss with the impetus to get back on his feet. Once there, something else occurred to him. A weapon. He needed a weapon. He still retained the knife on his belt, but that would be hopeless against any mounted assailants. Moaning with the effort required, he first checked the bodies of his own men. As expected, everything of use had been taken, even any money in their pockets. As he briefly surveyed the headshots that had killed them, anger again flared within him. That cockchafer Peck sure had a lot to answer for!

Moving on to the two rustlers that he had killed, Ewing suddenly got lucky. All their belt guns and knives had been removed, but not the double-barrelled Remington derringer tucked away in one of the cadaver's pants pocket. Digging deeper, he found half a dozen .41 calibre rimfire cartridges. That was all there was to be found, but at least he was no longer totally defenceless.

Finally, using his knife, he cut away a length of the cleanest shirtsleeve that he could find, which happened to be on one of his own men. Laboriously, he

wrapped it around his still bleeding wound and awkwardly tied it off. By this time he felt exhausted, but
there could be no help for that. His intention was to
attempt to intercept the chuck wagon before it
caught up with the herd. And, since the two men
were unlikely to be travelling at night, he stood a fair
chance . . . if he could stay on his feet. After a last, sad
glance at the bodies of his men, Ewing turned
towards the south-east and plodded off into the
apparently limitless gloom. It was time to find out
just how tough he really was!

Kiowa war parties came in all sizes. Some might
contain scores of warriors, whilst others could
amount to as few as two. The one that roamed north
of the Brazos that particular morning comprised the
latter. The only reason that they were able to travel
across the territory known to many as Comancheria
was because of their people's close affiliation to the
Comanche nation. No other Indians of the Southern
Plains had this bond. From their earlier home up
near the Missouri River, Kiowas had been driven
south by unrelenting pressure from the Sioux.
Having finally escaped the fiercest warriors on the
Northern Plains, they joined the Comanches in their
never-ending struggle with first the Mexicans and
then the Texans. It was a lone member of that second
grouping that the two 'horse Indians' now spied.

On foot and tottering, the solitary figure appeared
to be in bad shape. It was that fact that probably
saved his life . . . initially. The two young Kiowas cau-

tiously rode up behind him, watching closely. They well knew how dangerous Anglos could be when cornered. Finally they halted their ponies, glanced at each other and smiled gleefully. There was definitely some fun to be had with this one, especially as he was still unaware of their presence and didn't even seem to be armed.

The eldest of the two, whose slightly greater age entitled him to the first strike, hefted his vicious looking ball club in anticipation. The primitive weapon was basically a piece of rounded stone, wrapped in rawhide and securely attached to a hardwood handle. With sufficient force behind it, the club could easily shatter a man's skull, but his intention was to initially merely stun. A great deal of power could be gained by the sustained torture of a captured enemy. The very thought of that sent a thrill of excitement through him, and with a joyous whoop, he urged his pony into motion.

The white man's left shoulder was covered in dried blood, and so it was from that direction that the warrior approached. He was almost upon him before his stumbling victim realized it. The rush of unshod hoofs finally penetrated John Ewing's world of pain and fatigue, and at the last moment he defensively pitched forward. Hitting the ground, he groaned with pain, although it was debatable whether the worst of it came from the shoulder wound or the glancing blow that his head had just received.

The hard-riding Kiowa raced past, and then wheeled his mount around for another run. He howled out a warning to his companion that this was still his prey, and then readied his club for another swing. Before setting out, he checked one more time that the fallen Texan was still defenceless, and then surged forward.

As Ewing reached into a pocket for his derringer, a desperate will to live overcame both pain and fear. The hideously painted figure charging towards him was the stuff of nightmares, but it was still just flesh and blood. Cocking the over and under weapon, he resisted the strong urge to fire immediately. The .41 calibre handgun packed quite a punch but, favoured by cardsharps and prostitutes for its small size, its range was severely limited.

Because his victim lay on the ground, the warrior clung to the neck of his pony and with great skill swung down low to strike again. As a consequence, his whole body was in view. With scant yards to go, he raised his ball club for another great swing. It was then that the white man elevated his right hand. Unbelievably, there was a bright flash and a sudden shocking pain in the warrior's chest. As the animal carried him level with wounded Anglo, it was all the Kiowa could do to hang on. His fearsome club merely dragged uselessly over the grass as, by some quirk of fate, he then returned to the starting point next to his companion. That warrior managed to grab the reins and savagely brought the pony to a halt. It was at that point that the mortally wounded Indian's strength gave out. His grip loosened irrevocably, so that he ended up in a bloody heap next to his friend. That startled individual let go an enraged howl that again put the Texan on notice.

Ewing twisted painfully around just in time to witness the second warrior begin his own charge. 'Oh Christ!' he gasped. The diminutive pistol contained only one more cartridge, and there sure as hell wouldn't be any time for reloading! With his head throbbing, and his vision clouding, he finally managed to get the hammer retracted. The shrieking savage had got up to speed and was almost upon him. Shakily, Ewing tried to draw a bead on his attacker, but all he could really make out was the outline of the pony. There could be no help for it. That would just have to do. With the creature's hoofs almost upon him, he squeezed the trigger.

The derringer crashed out a second time, and this time its deadly load struck the chest of an animal rather than a human. Instinctively, Ewing kept on rolling to his right in a desperate attempt to get out of the path of the stricken beast. Although determined to keep on going, he nearly passed out as his injured shoulder inevitably took the strain. Groaning with agony, he didn't even possess the wherewithal to locate his assailant.

As his pony collapsed beneath him, the Kiowa flung himself from its back. He was young and agile, and hit the ground in a controlled roll, while still clutching his ball club. With the loss of both a friend and a valuable animal, he was consumed by raw hatred. This white man was going to suffer in ways that he couldn't even imagine.

Wracked by pain, Ewing nonetheless attempted to locate his enemy. Vaguely he discerned a human form spring lithely from the ground. Dropping the empty derringer, he grabbed his knife and swept it from side to side in front of him. The warrior, unhurt and confident of his abilities, regarded the shambling figure contemptuously for a moment before making his move. With dazzling speed, he raced forward and swung his club. The rawhide-covered head struck Ewing's blade with enough force to tear it from his grasp. Staggering back, he stared helplessly at his nemesis. He was played out, and he knew it!

Grinning savagely, the garishly daubed Indian advanced. He was going to enjoy this. Raising his club, he prepared to land a blow that would merely stun his victim, and so leave him available for every conceivable torment. The bullet that smashed into the Kiowa's back might as well have come from the moon, for all the warning either protagonist had of it. Then, as his knees buckled beneath him, the grin turned into a grimace that began to seep blood. The ball club, which seconds earlier had been so threatening, dropped meekly on to the grass.

John Ewing, still groggy and disorientated, didn't at first realize what had happened. It was only when he heard the sounds of a heavy wagon approaching that the possible reason for his survival dawned on him. The creaks and rattles were suddenly accompanied by Sam's great booming voice.

'You must have mighty big *cojones*, taking on two of

these devils with just a purse cannon and a tooth-pick!'

Ewing shook his head in joyous disbelief, but then immediately regretted it. As nausea overwhelmed him, he too dropped to his knees. There were hurried footsteps, and then the big teamster was by his side. 'It's OK, boss. We got you!'

Ewing clutched at his arm. He knew that he was about to pass out, but first he had something crucial to impart. 'Keep clear of the herd. Rustlers have it . . . and Peck's one of them!'

And then he was gone!

CHAPTER SEVEN

Sundown found the herd closing in on the northern border of the Lone Star State. The following day would see them crossing the Red River and on into the officially designated Indian Territory. On the face of it, all was going well for the rustlers . . . with one exception. As Vernon Peck yet again scrutinised their back trail, he muttered, 'Where in tarnation is that goddamned chuck wagon?'

Unless they had met with trouble, there was no good reason why the two men couldn't have repaired the wheel and caught up with them. He knew that, if necessary, the drovers and their captors could butcher a steer, but that would work out a mite costly if they had to do that for the remainder of the drive. Far better to locate the wagon . . . if it was still to be found.

'Come daybreak, I want you and Stiles to drop back and find that greaser cook and his *compadre*,' he remarked sombrely to another rustler by the name of Otis Price. 'Don't take any shit from them. If they want to see your bona fides, pop a cap on the team-ster. We can do without him. It's Montoya and his chuck wagon that we need.'

Price nodded agreeably. In truth, killing had never bothered him. 'If they're out there, we'll find them all right. An' I'd even kill for a decent cup of coffee right now, so the shooting part's not a problem.' With that, he urged his mount away to go off in search of Stiles.

Watching his crony depart, Peck morosely won-dered yet again whether the chuck wagon's non-appearance might have anything to do with John Ewing. Then he dismissed the idea as nonsense. It had definitely been a mistake not to kill his old army buddy, but the trail boss had been far too badly injured to intercept Sam and Montoya on foot. It was much more likely that they had either chosen to dawdle while off the leash, or run foul of Kiowas or Comanches or some such. As Price and Stiles would no doubt find out, *if* they did their job properly!

His eyes opened against painfully bright light and immediately closed again. Groaning, Ewing tugged a horse blanket up over his face and then tried again. That was better. Best to take it slowly. Then footfalls sounded nearby, and he tensed nervously.

'Who all's out there?' he croaked, his mouth dry as sun-baked rawhide.

'Easy, boss. Easy,' came Sam's reassuring tones. 'There ain't nobody about but me and Nico.'

Ewing heaved a sigh of relief and decided to

chance the sunlight again. Slowly he lowered the blanket. The teamster had considerately situated himself so that the injured man was now in his shadow. Peering cautiously about, the prone individual realized that from the location of the sun it had to be late morning. But *which* morning? Before he could attempt any more questions, the cook came into view holding a cup of coffee.

'Drink this, *jefe*. I make it *mucho* strong just for you.'

Alarm registered on the trail boss's features, and he struggled awkwardly into a sitting position. His freshly bandaged shoulder throbbed like the devil, but in truth not nearly as badly as before. Gazing around, he found that he was on a bedroll next to the big wagon. A small and relatively smokeless cooking fire burned nearby. Of the Kiowas there was no sign.

'After all that has happened, that fire is a mistake,' he rasped.

Montoya shook his head adamantly. 'If you are to get your strength back, you must eat. Hot food. Not just beef jerky and water.' With that, he returned to the fire to continue doing what he was paid for.

'Don't worry none about them heathen bastards,' Sam stated calmly. 'I put a ball into the other pony, so that when we left, there wasn't a single living thing left behind. The only way any of their *compadres* will find them is if they trip over them . . . and it's a big country.'

The teamster had done good, and Ewing nodded

his acknowledgement. But there was more on his mind than just roving war parties. 'That still leaves Peck. I know him. He will send people looking for you.'

As Montoya returned with a steaming plate full, Sam replied, 'I think you'd better tell the both of us what's been happening. But first you're gonna get this lot inside you. You might not know it, but you've been asleep for over twenty-four hours!'

With the irresistible aroma of bacon and beans in his nostrils, there could be no argument. John Ewing wolfed down the food like a starving man, which in truth was exactly what he was. Only when he had finally mopped up the grease and juice with biscuits, and belched loudly, did he tell his dire tale. Neither of the others made any comment until he had finished, and then it was Montoya who spoke first.

'That Peck! I knew he was trouble first I saw of him.' Patting his knife, he added, 'Should have aimed for his head, not the water barrel!'

Sam got to his feet and paced around. 'How do we know for sure that he took the herd? There were still plenty of Bar E hands left. They might have put up a fight.'

Ewing shook his head emphatically, and winced with the resultant pain. 'Oh he's got it all right. My old *friend* is a tricky son of a bitch, and there wasn't one single gunshot after he and his saddle tramps left me. And one thing else is for sure. They'll all be missing vittles such as these by now, which is why we have to be ready.'

Montoya still hadn't quite grasped the realities of their changed circumstances. '*Para qué?*' he queried in his native language.

'More killings,' his employer responded flatly. 'Only this time it'll be me drawing blood.' During the shocked silence that followed, he pondered on something. 'You've got a shotgun on that wagon.' It was more of a statement than a question. 'If we're gonna get through this mess, we got to act like this is war and get real mean. Just like the old days.' He glanced at Sam. 'Have you got the tools to cut a length of barrel off of his big gun?'

That man's eyes widened expressively. 'Well yeah, I guess.'

'So get to it. If I'm right, then we might not have long.'

The two rustlers, Stiles and Price, jogged along contentedly as their horses cantered across the open, brownish-green grassland. Apart from the almost perpetual wind, the weather provided little else to complain about. There wasn't a cloud in the sky, and the gruelling heat of summer hadn't yet arrived. They didn't consider it likely that their detached service would carry any particular dangers, and in truth were glad to be away from the stolen herd for the day. Vernon Peck always was an edgy bastard, but the unfamiliar responsibilities of controlling the progress of three thousand steers was not bringing out the best in him. Perhaps he would lighten up a bit once the chuck wagon had rejoined. And if the two men were instrumental in bringing that about, well so much the better for them.

For hour after hour they retraced the herd's path. A blind man on a galloping horse couldn't have missed its progress on the Chisholm Trail, but their task did involve sweeping from east to west, in case the wagon was following at the extremities of it. Then again, if all was well with the vehicle, it should easily have overhauled the others by then. And so, as the sun commenced its inevitable fall to the west, Stiles began to display signs of tension. He was a man of severe intellectual limitations, which of course was why he was merely acting as back up for his far more capable companion.

'You know, something just ain't right about all this,' he grumbled. As he spoke, dark tobacco juice trickled over his stubbly chin. What bothered him most was the prospect of the pair of them having to spend a night in a cold camp on the plains, because with Indians on the loose they sure couldn't risk lighting a fire. Suddenly their mission wasn't quite the soft option that it had earlier appeared. 'If that poxy cook was gonna to be located, we should have done it by now. Don't you reckon? Huh, huh?'

His companion wasn't really listening, because by divine timing Stiles's concerns were now no longer relevant. Off in the distance, Price had just spotted a single, large wagon. It was heading north, but sure as hell wasn't in any kind of hurry. 'Hush your moaning, and peel your eyes,' he retorted. 'We done found it, ain't we?'

The two searchers reined in and thoughtfully sat their mounts. It was definitely the same vehicle that they had seen when stalking the herd. Wide, high-sided, and pulled by a team of four mules, it was ambling along at a very leisurely pace. Two figures were just visible on the bench seat.

'What the hell are them pus weasels about?' Stiles growled. 'They're sure as shooting taking their own sweet time. Don't they realize there's a crew of drovers want feeding?'

'So let's go find out,' the other replied. 'And let's do it properly, just in case. We'll spread out, and come at them from either side. I'll do the talking. An' if we have to kill anyone, remember what I told you about the cook.'

Stiles was momentarily flummoxed. 'How will we know which is which? We've never seen them up close.'

Price sighed. He well knew why Peck had sent him along with Stiles. The tobacco-chewing peckerwood didn't even have the brains that God had given him. 'Because with a moniker like *Nico Montoya*, the cook just has to be some kind of greaser. Wouldn't you reckon?'

Stiles stared at him for a moment, before flashing a set of blackened teeth. 'Hot dang! You're pretty sharp, ain't you?'

The two men sat on the wide bench seat as though they hadn't a care in the world. Their mule team was being allowed to saunter along at a very leisurely pace, but looks could sometimes be deceiving.

'We got visitors,' Sam announced. 'Two white men, but none that I've ever seen before. An' they're coming in separately, on each flank, which means it ain't casual.'

'*Sí*, he's right,' Montoya added somewhat superfluously. 'What should we do, *jefe*?'

The response came from beneath them, on account of the fact that John Ewing was ensconced in the spacious wagon box underneath the seat. It wasn't the most comfortable place for a man with a wounded shoulder, but with a bedroll and blanket covering the board floor it had sufficed. 'Act hospitable,' he ordered. 'Like you've no idea who they are or what they're about. An' if it comes to gunplay, we can't allow either of them to escape. Savvy?'

Very aware of the Remington Army revolver digging in the small of his back, Sam nodded grimly. Then, belatedly realizing that Ewing couldn't see him, he replied, 'Oh yeah.'

The two rustlers had timed their approach pretty well. As Montoya cried out, 'Whoa there,' to his team, the horsemen reined in on either side of and just to the fore of the wagon. With Stiles still chewing away at his plug of tobacco, it was obvious that Price was to be the spokesman, and so it proved.

'Well how do there, fellas?' he began amiably enough.

'We're both mighty fine, an' I thank you for asking,' the big teamster replied with apparent good cheer. 'What brings you into these parts, friend?'

Otis Price regarded him indulgently. 'Well now, you mayn't know it, but we work for Mister Ewing of the Bar E. He's sent us down here to find out what might be ailing you, an' maybe chivvy you up a mite. His men are hankering for coffee and beans real bad.'

Sam's bluff features now registered puzzlement. 'I can understand that, but how come we ain't never seen you fellas before?'

Price was ready for that. 'Vernon Peck's a *compadre* of ours. Since your outfit's done lost a few drovers, Mister Ewing hired us on for the rest of the drive.' He paused, and then, all the while maintaining a friendly expression, continued with, 'Anyhu, we'll mosey along the rest of the way with you, an' you can just up the pace. Pronto!'

The teamster's smile remained in place, but a bleak chill came into his eyes. 'What if I was to say I didn't believe you?'

Despite being warned to keep his mouth shut, Stiles just couldn't help himself. 'Which bit?' he enquired, because it had all sounded pretty convincing to him.

Even as his simple companion spoke, Price's right hand began to drift towards the revolver at his waist. And yet, even though possessing a keen 'nose' for danger, the gun thug could not possibly have anticipated the next occurrence. From beneath the bench seat, and between the legs of its two occupants, appeared the gaping muzzles of a sawn-off shotgun.

'The *bit* about Mister Ewing,' came a rather disembodied response.

Before he could even contemplate drawing a weapon, Stiles's jaw dropped comically, and so he was spared the shattering destruction of the twelve-gauge. Not so his companion. As the big gun swung his way, Price had a split second to choose his fate, and as ever with his kind he favoured violence. With practised speed, his Colt cleared gun leather. As the hammer came back, he was already swinging sideways out of his saddle in a bid to escape the dreadful blast. His revolver lined up on a point just below the wooden seat, and it was touch and go as to who would get off the first shot. Sadly for Otis Price it proved to be the hidden shooter, and one was all it took.

Accompanied by a ferocious muzzle flash, the shotgun's murderous discharge threw out a load of jagged metal at the rustler's brutalised features, totally obliterating them. As the lifeless body continued its now uncontrolled plunge from the saddle, its forefinger squeezed the trigger reflexively. The ball missed its intended target, but by an appalling stroke of luck the hot lead quite literally blew out the brains of Price's horse. Without a sound, the luckless beast collapsed to the ground next to its erstwhile owner.

Because of his position on the opposite flank, Stiles had not actually witnessed his partner's gory demise, but even his slow mind made the connection. His choice then was to fight or flee, and as had Price before him he chose the former. The rustler was no slouch with a six-gun, but from his position on the left of the bench seat, Sam already had a cocked Remington in his right hand. Swinging it around from behind his back, all he had to do was squeeze the trigger. The heavy ball punched a bloody hole in his opponent's chest, causing the rustler to sway back in the saddle. Stiles's gun hand suddenly flopped loosely by his side, so that the weapon was pointing harmlessly at the grass.

Awkwardly appearing from beneath the seat, Ewing peered from right to left. A cursory glance confirmed that his own victim was most definitely very dead . . . and completely unrecognizable. The other fellow still retained his gun, but then even as the three men watched, it slid from fingers that no longer possessed any strength. Having handed his shotgun to Montoya, and aided by the teamster, Ewing clambered out of the box and down to the ground so that he could approach the mounted outlaw. Probably because it still had a rider, that man's horse had remained in place.

With blood soaking his shirt, Stiles was still breathing, but only just. It came in short, wheezing gasps, and with each out-take tobacco juice flowed over his lower jaw. Grunting from the effort, Ewing bent down and recovered the revolver. It was a very clean and obviously well maintained Colt Army, and he nodded with satisfaction. Its owner was a scruffy-looking cuss, but he had looked after his weapon, and it would make an ideal replacement for the gun taken by Peck. Instinctively feeling less vulnerable,

Ewing eased it into his empty holster.

'Were any more of my hands killed?' he demanded of the dying man.

Stiles's head now lolled to one side, and he appeared unable to focus on his inquisitor. 'Eh?' was all he could manage.

Ewing shook his head in disgust and seized the reins. Suddenly aware that Sam was by his side, he said, 'Tip him out of that saddle before he bleeds all over it and then tether this animal to the back of the wagon. We might have use of it where we're going.'

There was a thump as Stiles's body hit the ground. As Ewing moved over to the other rustler's corpse, he called up to the cook. 'Has that shooting attracted any attention?'

Montoya gave a start, as though coming to his senses. Although well used to life on a cattle drive, he had not really encountered a great deal of bloody violence . . . until then. The sight of Price's gruesome demise had undeniably given him pause. Clambering to his feet on the wagon, he took a careful look around. 'No, senor. There is no one out there . . . that I can see.'

Ewing grunted. He supposed that that would have to do. One never knew who might be over the horizon, and so all they could do was take their chances.

With their newly acquired animal following on behind, and Price's saddle and weapons stashed in the wagon, it was time to move on. As Montoya urged his team into movement, Ewing glanced coldly down at Stiles from his position on the bench seat. The stricken outlaw was still emitting short gasps.

'Don't seem quite right leaving him like that,' Sam muttered softly next to him.

When Ewing turned to the teamster that man detected a harder edge to him. Something that he hadn't noticed before. Maybe it had always been there, but concealed under a veneer of civilization, or maybe it had grown out of his recent experiences. Either way, it was amply demonstrated by his next comment.

'He stays where he lays. Let him bleed out, 'cause I sure ain't wasting powder and lead on the likes of him!'

With nothing more to say on that subject, it was Nico Montoya who asked the inevitable question. 'What do you intend us to do, *jefe*? What is your plan?'

Ewing's chill expression moderated some as he responded. 'We'll do what those damned rustlers did to us. We'll shadow them and wait for an opportunity. The herd will likely be up into Indian Territory by now. That's full of thieves and renegades. Vernon Peck may well find that keeping hold of those cattle is not as easy as stealing them in the first place. He made a big mistake letting me live, and I'm gonna make him regret it. And if all else fails, then there's one thing he won't have considered.'

Both men stared at him curiously, but it was Sam who spoke first. 'And just what might that be, boss?'

Despite the seriousness of the situation, Ewing couldn't resist favouring them both with a broad smile. 'Why, Texas Fever, of course!'

CHAPTER EIGHT

'So *what* are you gonna do about them, Marshal?' The loud voice from over by the threshold of the jail-house was authoritarian and insistent.

Tom 'Bear River' Smith glanced up from his desk and sighed. An experienced lawman, having served in, amongst other places, New York City and Bear River, Wyoming, he had known without looking who it was, and also the nature of the man's business. But he wasn't going to make it easy for him.

'*Them* being?' he queried.

'The goddamned Confederate cattle, of course,' Jacob Stone retorted. He was a big man with an even bigger opinion of himself, who unfortunately just happened to be one of the largest landowners in the state of Kansas. And he had one very particular subject on his mind. 'There'll be herds moving up that Chisholm Trail again, now that spring is here. An' they'll all be carrying tick fever.'

'You say,' the marshal responded provocatively.

'Yeah, I say!' Stone barked, slamming the jailhouse

door behind him. It was obvious that there was far more to come, and he didn't disappoint. 'Those Texas steers carry disease. You know it and I know it. If any of them get in amongst my animals it'll cost me dear. An' I ain't in business to lose money.'

Smith tilted back his chair and regarded the rancher evenly. In truth, he wasn't entirely unsympathetic. It was just his visitor's abrasive manner to which he took objection. A half smile appeared under the peace officer's heavy, drooping moustache. 'So what is it you want me to do?'

Stone was building up quite a head of steam. 'Since no one's thought fit to appoint a county sheriff yet, you carry the law in these parts. So any herd that turns up, you just send them on their way. To anywhere that's *not* Dickinson County. Then they become someone else's problem.'

Shaking his head, the lawman patted the brass badge pinned to his jacket. 'I'm appointed by the city fathers to maintain order in Abilene. If those Texan drovers try to run their herd down Main Street, I'd have to take issue with them. As it is, McCoy's stockyards are beyond the city limits . . . and so outside my jurisdiction.' He paused, and then before the other man could object added, 'Believe me when I tell you that my life would be a lot easier without these Texas hoorahs coming up here every year, but they also spend an awful lot of money in town. Which is why you've come to me, ain't it? The mayor just wasn't interested!'

The rancher bristled with frustrated anger. 'If I

was of a mind, I could see to it that your job got a lot harder, Smith!'

Something about the marshal's demeanour changed abruptly. There was no longer the trace of a smile as he got to his feet and strode around the desk. His movements were controlled and athletic, and he emanated an aura of raw physical power. When he was about two feet away from his visitor he stopped. Slowly he drew in a deep breath and balled his large fists.

'Don't ask for considerations and then threaten me in the same breath, *Mister* Stone.'

Despite his own considerable bulk, that individual suddenly regarded the unarmed, but cold-eyed lawman warily. He well knew that Tom Smith had been a boxer in times past, and that during his short spell in Abilene he had preferred to enforce the law with his fists rather than hot lead. The broad shoulders and confident stance all indicated a man who could handle trouble. His positioning opposite his opponent was no accident. If the larger man tried anything, Smith was just at the right distance to unleash a flurry of well-aimed blows. And Jacob Stone was no fool. He didn't fancy being knocked cold and then waking up behind bars, an object of amusement for the whole town.

'OK. You win,' he rasped angrily. 'For now. But if the law won't help me, I'll have to stop those damn southerners myself. And trouble has a habit of spreading.'

Marshal Smith regarded him impassively. 'Well I'll

be ready and waiting if any of it should spread into my town. So long, Mister Stone.'

Vernon Peck irritably spat a stream of phlegm into the long grass. This trail-driving shit really was something else, and none of it good. It seemed as though everybody and everything needed watching like a hawk. After a brief stop at Red River Station, a small community on the south bank of the watercourse, the herd had crossed over into the only part of the United States that was officially designated as Indian Territory. It had struck him at the time that the latter name was really something of a misnomer, since there was no lack of damn savages elsewhere in the country. Anyhu, lulled into a false sense of security by the sand bar shelving out from the north bank, some of the less experienced drovers had got careless and a number of steers had been swept away by the unexpectedly strong current. At over forty dollars a head, the new boss had not been best pleased!

And where the hell were the chuck wagon, and the two men that he'd sent out to find it? If it was ever going to turn up, then it should surely have done so. Stiles was unquestionably a meathead, but Price was more than capable of handling such a task . . . unless they'd run into more trouble than they could handle. Briefly he contemplated sending out another search party, but then decided against it. His original twelve sidekicks had been whittled down to seven able-bodied men. On the plus side that meant fewer shares to be divvied up, especially if Breck's foot chose to infect and claimed his miserable life. But with dangerous territory up ahead, he couldn't afford to risk losing any more of his gun thugs. So they would all just have to accept the loss of the poxy cook and his supplies, and live off slaughtered steers and any creatures that were unlucky enough to come under their guns. All other luxuries, such as coffee, would have to wait until they returned to what passed for civilization on the frontier.

One of the few positives was that Ewing's drovers and wranglers had proved to be surprisingly acquiescent. Knowing that he couldn't hope to control them all the way to Kansas by threats alone, Peck had promised them that following the sale of the cattle in Abilene they would not only receive their full pay, but also an extra fifty dollars per man. Their mostly cheerful acceptance of his terms proved just how short some people's memories could be. It didn't seem to have occurred to the trail hands that their new employer wasn't really someone they could trust . . . with anything. But then again, they hadn't actually witnessed his brutal slaying of their comrades.

Unfortunately, there was something bothering the gunhand far more than just the various responsibilities of overseeing the whole operation. Something that might affect everybody on the drive. It was indefinable, but nonetheless troubling. A sixth sense, developed over years of wrongdoing, told him that the herd was being watched. He grunted at the irony of such a situation. Having stolen another man's cattle, there was now a possibility that some other *hombres* were planning to attempt the same thing with him.

The vast area of the west known as Indian Territory was home to members of every tribe ever banished beyond the Mississippi. Mostly unwilling victims of the 1830 Removal Act and all the subsequent expulsions of the following decades, they included many warriors who weren't prepared to embrace a downtrodden role in exchange for often non-existent rations and subsidies promised by the US Government. Their numbers included Cherokees, Chickasaws, Choctaws, Creeks, Osages, Seminoles and Shawnees. More recently they had been joined by Arapahos, Cheyennes, Comanches and Kiowas seeking to escape the US Army's ever increasing punitive expeditions.

The rag-tag group that had been surreptitiously shadowing the large herd since it had crossed the Red River was an unholy mixture of horse Indians and white renegades. The latter trash had started out as whiskey peddlers, but when their supplies of the watered down Kansas 'sheep-dip' temporarily ran out they decided to stick around for a while and look for other opportunities. Utilising a mixture of bastardized English and sign language, the leader of the white element had just got through explaining his plan to the score or so sorry-looking warriors that were hunkered down nearby.

'So what d'you reckon, Flint? Are the sons of bitches up for it?' one of his men queried hopefully.

That man grunted, before hawking up a stream of yellow phlegm. Then, keeping his voice low, he replied, 'The tarnal curs wanted to try for the whole herd, but that's just plain foolish. With upwards of thirty guns riding with it, there ain't enough of us to take on the whole outfit. Far better to cut out a couple of hundred head when we get the right weather for it. Odds are, they'll just accept the loss and continue on their way. Coming up the Chisholm Trail, it likely won't be the first time they've had to pay tribute to dirt worshippers for right of way.'

The outlaw nodded to himself, infinitely satisfied with his plan. Millard Flint was a thoroughly unwholesome character, but he did possess enough intelligence to be more than just casually dangerous. And with his brutalised features covered in smallpox scars, and a gunpowder burn near his right eye, his appearance more than matched his dubious reputation.

His half-dozen dog-eared cronies shrugged their agreement. Now that the whiskey had run out, they all relished the prospect of returning to one of Kansas's frontier cow towns. Myriad saloons and whorehouses awaited them, and with what they already had in their pokes plus the anticipated sale proceeds of some stolen cattle, they could look forward to a welcome period of debauchery.

'So when do we do it?' one of them demanded impatiently.

Flint regarded him balefully. 'When I say, you god-damned cockchafer!' Then, relenting slightly, he

101

added, 'Most likely the next cloudy night. Makes sense to avoid gunplay if we can.'

Nearly one whole week had passed since the Red River crossing, and the minor, but nevertheless constant gnawing in Vernon Peck's guts had never left him. The veracity of his instinct appeared to have been confirmed a day earlier, when sunlight had momentarily reflected from something in the distance. And now the weather was turning. The near constant wind remained, but the clear blue skies had been replaced by threatening cloud formations. If there were some hard cases lurking out there, and they were ever going to make a move, it would very likely be that night.

Yet in truth, neither Peck nor any of his men had actually seen anyone acting suspicious. For sure, Indians of one tribe or another had been spotted, but on perceiving the number of trail hands accompanying the herd they had drifted off, without having made any attempt to hide their presence. It was the varmints that he hadn't seen that bothered the new trail boss!

His intuitive certainty that something was soon to happen presented Peck with a new dilemma. Should he arm Reno and his drovers, or should he rely on his own dwindling gang of gun thugs? Having pondered long and hard, he decided to take the latter course. Although Ewing's crew appeared to have accepted his ascendancy, it was also the case that they far outnumbered his own men. With six-guns strapped to their waists again, there could be no telling what might happen.

Mind made up, Peck began a circuit of the herd, reining in next to each of his six mounted ruffians in turn so that he could quietly alert them to what the night might bring. At no point did he mention his suspicions to any of Reno's men. He ended up alongside Sam's wagon, which was now serving a multitude of purposes. In addition to newly born calves, it contained all the drovers' weapons and an increasingly despondent Josiah Breck, whose wounded foot had finally begun to 'turn'.

Having explained the situation to his temporary teamster, the gang leader, weighed down by unforeseen responsibilities, peered impatiently over at the tormented gun thug in the rear of the wagon bed. His damaged boot had long since been discarded, and the putrid wreckage of his foot was on display for all to see. Peck's nose wrinkled with distaste. For Breck to have any chance of survival, the whole foot would have to come off, and his boss really didn't feel any inclination to bother with all that. After all, nobody had asked the dumb bastard to get himself shot!

'If it comes to trouble, can you handle a gun?' he demanded brusquely.

The injured man stared up at him through painwracked eyes and mumbled something totally incomprehensible. Peck grunted with disgust. So no help there then. It would therefore be up to the eight of them to fend off whatever came at them in the night.

Millard Flint nodded with satisfaction. As expected, and for the first time in weeks, the darkness was nearly complete. It meant that a clear advantage lay with those who knew the terrain. Quite deliberately, he had split his forces. The dissolute Indians, who included both Comanches and Kiowas, had been assigned the task of cutting out and running off a small portion of the herd. Their carefully nurtured need for whiskey, which they could only obtain from white men, meant that that night at least they would do as requested. And even though no longer the consummate warriors that they had been, stealing livestock was still something they excelled at.

Flint and his renegades were to create a diversion, but nothing too noisy. It served no one's purposes for there to be a full-blown stampede.

'Remember,' he hissed at the others. 'No shooting. We gut one of the nighthawks, so that he gets to wailing some. Just enough to attract his compadres. When they come running, we simply back off. Savvy?'

His cronies grunted their agreement. They had no interest in getting into a gunfight with a bunch of trigger-happy drovers. If anyone was to be shot full of lead, at least let it be a worthless savage!

'Right. Let's move out,' Flint whispered. And so they did.

'What the hell's up with you fellas?' Mesquite Bill demanded of their captors, as he lay sprawled out on his bedroll. It was fully dark, and all the hands had eaten. Of all the Bar E drovers, he was the one who had most resented the violent replacement of their employer. In his opinion John Ewing had seemed like a decent and honourable man. 'Seems like you've done sat on an anthill,' he added sourly.

His was indeed a pretty apt description, because Peck and his seven men were all prowling restlessly around the perimeter of the camp, just beyond the immediate firelight. Their problem was that, since the herd was spread out over a vast area, they couldn't possibly know where any rustlers might strike. Therefore all they could do was be prepared to react at the first sound of a disturbance. And as it happened, that wasn't long in coming.

As usual there were two nighthawks patrolling the herd's outer limits. Since one was travelling clockwise and the other counter-clockwise, it meant that they encountered each other on two occasions during each cycle. Anyone waiting to attack them individually only had to keep watch for a time to work out their schedule, and that was exactly what happened.

Dan Adams' night vision was fully adapted to the conditions, but since he had no inkling of possible trouble, his attention was quite rightly on the herd. It was also a fact that, other than the small knife on his belt, he was completely unarmed. Realizing gratefully that his shift couldn't have much longer to run, he was looking forward to some well-earned shuteye. And with the cattle continuing to graze peacefully, there was every sign that it would be a quiet night.

The first and only intimation of trouble came when he perceived hurried footfalls behind him. Since no cowman ever walked anywhere, it couldn't be any of his *compadres*. Thoroughly alarmed, he rapidly twisted round in the saddle. As the drover made out a number of dark forms closing on him rapidly, a thrill of real horror flashed through him. Instinctively, his hand streaked to the non-existent sidearm at his waist, when what he should have done was sink his heels in. By the time he realized his mistake it was too late.

As something very long and sharp lunged at him, an overwhelming pain assailed Dan's flat stomach. Doubling over, a loud moan escaped his lips, and then someone grabbed hold of his left arm. Unable to resist, he was dragged to the ground. To ensure that they were definitely overheard, Flint brutally twisted the knife, and was rewarded with an agonised groan that was more than loud enough to travel.

'That should answer,' he muttered to the others, while extracting the greasy blade. It finally came clear of the punctured flesh with an unpleasant sucking sound that was music to his ears. He was known as a man who took pleasure in his work. 'I'd say it's time to hightail it, boys,' he added. But in truth he was taken by surprise at the speed of the drovers' response.

'That weren't no goddamned steer,' Peck snarled, and like chain lightning he raced off into the night, to be followed rather more slowly by his startled men. With a Colt in each hand, he charged through the gloom towards the source of the strange sounds. *Charged* wasn't strictly accurate, because he had to thread his way through the herd, but suddenly he spotted a riderless horse. More cautiously, the gunhand closed in until two more visions became apparent.

A man lay on the ground, squirming like an impaled snake, and just beyond him was a single figure disappearing into the darkness. Coming to a snap decision, Peck levelled his right-hand Colt and fired. The resulting crash and muzzle flash seemed to rend the night, and he could only fervently hope, pray not being a word that could ever apply to him, that the cattle wouldn't stampede. Ahead of him, the unknown fugitive cried out and pitched sideways.

'Fan out,' he yelled to the others coming up behind him. 'An' no more shooting unless you have to.'

Although the cattle nearest to them were shifting uneasily, the animals didn't appear inclined to take flight just yet. Guns at the ready, Peck first checked on the drover. That individual was obviously fading fast, and now lay like a stranded whale, twitching and moaning as his lifeblood drained away. 'Help me!' he croaked.

The trail boss favoured him with a cursory examination before stating coldly, 'Cain't do nothing for you, son. Best you just lay quiet and bleed out.' With that, he swiftly moved on to the man that he had shot, who was now surrounded and disarmed by his men. Yet before Peck could say or do anything further, the sound of joyous whoops and then the pounding of many hoofs in the distance forestalled him.

'Goddamn it all to hell!' he managed finally. 'Someone's going to pay dearly for this night's work.'

CHAPTER NINE

Despite the very real danger involved, the wild ride north-west across the darkened landscape had been strangely exhilarating. It had been forced on Flint and his remaining men because there was no way he could allow the Indians to simply disappear with the stolen cattle, which they could well have done if he hadn't turned up quickly at the rendezvous.

'Who've we lost?' he barked out, as they finally dismounted in the concealed arroyo.

For a few moments all was confusion. The Texas Longhorns, tired and winded after the enforced stampede, were milling around nearby. The exultant warriors were whooping around them deliriously. Somehow, stealing livestock from the white eyes was even more enjoyable when assisted by members of that same race.

'Has to be Gates,' one of his men responded breathlessly. 'Bastards shot him in the back. Went straight down, like a sack of meal. Dead as a wagon tyre, for sure.' In truth, he had no idea what had happened to the missing man, but he had no intention of going back to look for him and so, not for the first time in his miserable life, had resorted to a tall tale. And after all, there *had* been a gunshot.

'You saw this?' Flint demanded fiercely. He well knew that any man could be made to talk, and he didn't want any loose ends.

'Damn right I did,' retorted the supposed eyewitness, thereby proving that lies could really only be compounded on.

Millard Flint drew in a deep, steadying breath before finally nodding. 'OK. Fair enough. So we'll rest up here 'til daybreak before moving on.' He glanced over at the darkened mass of men and animals. 'I'll go and square things with the dirt worshippers. A *little* cash on account, since they won't be coming to Kansas with us. Ha.' Chuckling happily, he made his way over to the still celebrating Indians. In a way, it was a shame about Gates. He'd been a good man, but his demise did mean that there was one less to share in the spoils. So all in all, it had been a reasonably passable night's work!

'You an' me are gonna have a little talk,' Vernon Peck remarked softly to their grievously wounded prisoner. Pretty much everything said and thought about Ben Gates had been true ... except the bit about his demise. Although to look at him, that surely wouldn't be far off.

'Water,' that man pleaded. He lay on the trampled

grass between a campfire and the wagon. Blood soaked his jacket, and he was obviously in a bad way. The presence of a fellow sufferer had even penetrated Breck's world of hurt. That miserable wretch clung to the wagon side, so as to get a better view of the entertainment. Along with his fellow gun thugs, there were also most of the trail hands, thereby constituting a sizeable audience. Ewing's men, having recovered Dan Adams's body, were angry, and not just with his murderers. But any other recriminations would have to wait until the present business had been settled.

'Water, is it?' scoffed Peck. He affected to ponder for a few seconds before responding. 'So that must mean you want to trade. OK, fair enough. I give you water, you tell me what I want to know.' Clicking his fingers for a canteen, he waited until it was in his hands before dropping down onto his haunches next to the suffering rustler.

'Where will I find your *compadres*?'

Although in terrible pain, Gates retained sufficient wit to realize that he only had one chance. 'Water!' he insisted.

Peck's eyes narrowed dangerously for a moment, before he suddenly favoured his victim with a cold smile. 'Oh yeah,' he muttered, before upending the canteen over Gates' face.

The dying man choked and gasped, but then his eyes widened in shock as a knifepoint appeared before them. Looming behind it were the lean, hard features of his interrogator.

'From the look of the nighthawk that you fellas killed, one of your pardners obviously liked playing with knives. Maybe it was you. Who knows? I don't really give a shit. But one thing's for sure, I ain't gonna ask you again.'

Any more thoughts of bargaining were quickly forgotten. 'Indians and whites riding together. Off to the north-east a ways,' Gates mumbled painfully. 'There's a big arroyo.'

'How far a ways?'

The rustler struggled with that. He was weakening fast. 'T . . .two hours . . . ride,'

'Now that wasn't so difficult, was it?' Peck responded mildly, before plunging the blade deep into Gates' throat. With even his own men looking on aghast, the trail boss snarled out,' No one steals from me. No one!'

That was followed by a long silence, which was finally broken by a bitterly unhappy, and surprisingly bold, Mesquite Bill. 'You knew there would be trouble tonight, you bastard, yet you never warned us,' he accused. 'And now Dan's been paroled to Jesus.'

Peck regarded him bleakly. 'What difference would it have made if you'd known? We couldn't be everywhere at once. And it wouldn't have mattered whether it was me or John Ewing running this outfit. Those sons of bitches would still have made a try for the herd.'

'Except that Dan could have been packing a hog leg, you bull turd,' Bill retorted. 'As it was, he was defenceless!'

Vernon Peck dropped the bloodied knife and rose to his feet. His features had gone taut again, as though in a prelude to yet more violence. 'You really don't want to press me, mister. Else there'll be another drover short.'

Reno's voice came from the sidelines. 'Is it your intention to pursue them rustlers?'

'That it is,' Peck replied, although his hard eyes never left Bill.

'Well then, let some of us come with you. Give us our long guns back, an' we'll side with you against the renegades. It was our man they killed, not yours. And it sounded like there could be more than enough of them to go around.'

Peck thought for a moment. The idea made sense, because he didn't have enough men to both take on the outlaws and supervise the herd and drovers. And one way or another he needed to act fast. 'Agreed. Two of my men will come along, and they'll keep your guns until we locate this arroyo.' He raised his voice a touch. 'The rest of you will move the herd at first light. We'll all be going in roughly the same direction anyhu.'

'And we get to bury Dan,' Reno pressed.

'Whatever,' Peck responded with obvious disinterest. 'And you will be one of those coming with us,' he added, nodding at Bill. 'I want you where I can see you.' Turning away, he moved briskly towards his horse.

'What about my foot, Vern?' Breck enquired plaintively.

'What about it?' that man replied without even breaking step.

The Godless heathens had departed during the night, no doubt taking a few steers with them by way of additional recompense. But not too many, because they wanted to remain on good terms with the whiskey traders. And as it turned out, with the coming of daylight, there still appeared to be well in excess of two hundred animals scattered around the camp. The Indians had done good, but the renegades had done far better! Even after they had whooped it up in Kansas, the remaining sale proceeds would buy plenty of watered down whiskey to bring back into Indian Territory. So it was that Millard Flint had a warm feeling in his gut that didn't just relate to the hot coffee swilling about in it.

Deciding that it was time they were on their way, he glanced up from the small cooking fire with the intention of rousting out his cronies. Coincidentally, his gaze drifted back towards the south-west and he suddenly beheld a strange and unsettling sight. A lone rider was approaching steadily along the arroyo. The newcomer held a rifle canted upright, with the butt resting on his thigh. What appeared to be a once white shirt was tied to the barrel. Flint's brow furrowed as he pondered the vexing development.

'Get on your feet, you lazy bastards,' he growled. 'Seems like someone wants a parley.'

His eight men, struggling to shake off the effects of sleep, peered around in alarm. Although only one stranger was visible, that didn't mean there weren't others. Their leader slowly stood up, loosened the revolver in its holster, and then barked out, 'Some of you get over by the horses, an' stay with them until I know who we're dealing with. Make sure they're well tethered. And all of you keep your eyes peeled. We ain't the only ones outlawed up in this territory.'

Vernon Peck kept his lean features impassive as he advanced on the assorted ruffians and *their* cattle. As always when bloody violence was imminent, a mixture of emotions assailed him, but none of them showed on his face. His watchful eyes took in the apparent leader, and he knew that come what may that man would have to die. Unsurprisingly it was that individual who happened to speak first.

'That'll be far enough, mister. At least until I know your intentions.'

Peck reined in his animal obligingly, but then rather than introduce himself he just sat there silently, without even blinking. Flint, never a man to be trifled with, began to feel anger surge through his body.

'State your business *now* or get to dying,' he snarled, as his right hand moved towards the holstered revolver.

Peck tilted his head slightly to one side, as though attempting to come to terms with a strange notion. 'Stealing stolen cattle,' he remarked. 'All of my life, I've never heard of such a thing!'

Flint blinked, his confusion obvious. 'Say what?'

115

Peck uttered a theatrical sigh, as though dealing with an awkward child. '*What* I'm saying is, I killed to steal those steers, and I'll kill to keep them.' Before the final words were out of his mouth, he allowed the muzzle of his cocked Winchester to drop to the horizontal and then squeezed the trigger.

To give him his due, Flint was no slouch with a gun. He had cleared leather before the bullet penetrated his chest. The shocking pain prevented any further movement, and yet bizarrely he did not fall. Instead he merely stood there helplessly, as all hell broke loose around him.

Peck, knowing that in his position survival was all about movement, allowed the Winchester to fall from his grasp. Then, drawing both Colts, he urged his mount into motion and sped off to his right. It was then that his hidden back-up opened fire. They had crawled into position before dawn on his left flank. Concealed behind some scrubby bushes that were kept in existence by the occasional flash flood, they opened fire with their long guns.

Most of Flint's remaining men dropped to the ground in confusion, except for one man who decided to take his chances on horseback. With no inclination to spend time securing a saddle, he merely leapt on to the nearest animal and raced precariously away. Mesquite Bill made his flight a whole lot rougher by sending a piece of lead into the fugitive's left shoulder. The last anyone saw of him was doubled over, heading in a vaguely southerly direction at speed.

Peck possessed the natural instincts of a guerrilla fighter. By deliberately riding into the midst of the Longhorns, he therefore became invisible to his recumbent foes. With both Colts cocked, he carefully threaded his way through the cattle, taking great care to avoid any contact with their horns. Flint's remaining cronies were returning their attackers' fire, when really they should have been watching their rear. That was where the real danger lay.

The mounted pistol fighter appeared behind them and immediately began to wreak bloody havoc. Alternating with first one revolver and then the next, Vernon Peck fired down into the terrified rustlers. One took a ball to the head, which burst open like a ripe melon. Another received a piece of hot lead in his lower back as he desperately attempted to crawl to safety. The three rustlers over by their horses were unable to assist as they too were under heavy fire.

Knowing better than to stay in one place, Peck kept his horse constantly on the move to minimize the risk, but he had just gut shot his penultimate opponent when his own luck ran out. The remaining outlaw got off a lucky shot that slammed into the underside of his horse's belly. Screaming in agony, the poor creature began to topple sideways, so that its rider only just managed to roll clear. With savage bloodlust coursing through his body, Peck rapidly drew a bead on the horse killer. With a consummate display of shooting, his first ball penetrated neatly between the eyes, only to be followed by another that lifted off part of the dead man's skull.

Nearby, the tethered horses no longer had any guards capable of drawing breath. Out-positioned and outgunned, those men had died in a welter of blood and gore. All of which meant that the cattle had now been effectively repossessed by the original thieves.

The jubilant Bar E drovers were suddenly confronted by Vernon Peck striding towards them, both his smoking Colt Navy's unwaveringly covering them.

'You done good, fellas. Real good,' that man remarked. 'But now I want all them guns in the dirt.'

'You really are all shit an' no sugar, Vernon Peck,' retorted an aggrieved Mesquite Bill.

The other man's features hardened as a certain memory came to him. He also had uttered those same words, only to John Ewing at the start of the drive. Momentarily he wondered just what had become of him . . . but only momentarily. Gesturing sharply with one of his revolvers, he stated flatly, 'That's just the way it is, fella. Now drop 'em!'

Muttering unhappily, the trail hands reluctantly surrendered their weapons. Only then did Peck holster one of his weapons as he turned to survey the carnage. Of those that he had personally shot, only the leader remained on his feet, which was bizarre in itself. Drifting closer to inspect him, the corners of Peck's mouth turned up in something approaching a smile. This really was the darnedest thing. The outlaw boss appeared to be quite literally dead on his feet. The revolver in his right hand had slipped to the ground. His eyes were half-closed and his breathing had stopped.

'Give the sad cuss a shove, Vern,' suggested one of his men gleefully. 'On account of maybe he's dead, but doesn't know it. Haw, haw, haw.'

Peck glanced at his dying horse, and anger again flared. That had been a damn good mount. The muzzle of his Colt jabbed forward sharply and Millard Flint, very definitely deceased, fell back and down, to land with a thud in the long grass. As his men checked on the other cadavers for weapons and loot, their boss sighed and drew his knife.

For a moment, Mesquite Bill actually thought that the gunhand intended scalping his victim to obtain a keepsake, but then watched as he instead moved purposefully away to put his animal out of its misery. As the Bar E hand watched him complete the gory task, it occurred to him that this man was quite probably capable of killing his own mother . . . if he hadn't already.

Job done, Peck returned briefly to Flint's corpse to wipe his bloody hands and knife clean on the man's clothing. Then his gimlet eyes surveyed their surroundings.

'We've wasted enough time on these low-lifes,' he opined to his two cronies. 'Collect up everything that's worth anything and get the horses. We've got some steers to move. We'll divvy up once we rejoin the herd.' With that, he recovered his saddle and went looking for the best of their victims' horses. When all was said and done, it had still been a profitable morning!

*

Even though none of the three men were experienced readers of sign, the abandoned campsite had quite a tale to tell . . . and not all of it good. Near the burnt-out fire there lay a blood-soaked corpse that thankfully was unknown to them. Unfortunately, the same couldn't be said for the occupant of the hastily dug, unmarked grave.

'Goddamn it all to hell!' John Ewing exclaimed, as he stared down at what had once been Dan Adams. They had scooped away most of the shallow covering, but even coated with particles of soil, it was still painfully obvious how he had died. 'Peck's got a lot to answer for,' he added bitterly.

And yet, some time later, after they had spread out and carefully examined the surrounding terrain, a different story became apparent. 'Seems to me, boss,' Sam remarked thoughtfully. 'That we weren't the only outfit shadowing the herd. Very likely Dan was killed by one of this new bunch of rustlers, and then one of them was shot in the back hightailing it.'

Ewing nodded as he unconsciously massaged his aching shoulder. The wound was healing well, but it still had some way to go. 'I reckon you've got the right of it. And whoever they are ran off a couple of hundred head.' He suddenly favoured the others with a bleak smile. 'Which means Vern ain't having things all his own way.'

Montoya had resurrected the campfire to prepare some coffee, but that wasn't the only thing he had to offer. 'Not all the rustlers' animals had shod hoofs, *jefe.*'

Ewing's brow furrowed. 'White men riding with savages. I didn't think Comancheros would come this far east.'

'Mayhap they're whiskey peddlers,' Sam suggested. 'Those bastards'll turn their hand to anything that'll show a profit.'

For a few moments they sat quietly in the shade of the chuck wagon, sipping hot coffee and mulling over the turn of events. In recent days, Ewing had got to know his two employees far better, and had developed a genuine liking and affection for them. In their case, although wary of his grim desire for revenge, they had stated their intention to stay with him come what may. And that resolve was soon to be tested.

'Rider coming in from the north,' Sam announced suddenly. 'Looks like he's hurting.'

John Ewing reached for the roughly modified shotgun. Since its baptism of fire, Montoya had not evinced any desire to have it back. 'Now who might this be?' Then he frowned. 'One thing's for sure. He's running from something.'

Nico Montoya glanced at him curiously. 'How can you tell, *jefe?*'

Sam grunted. With their boss now checking the seating of the sawn-off's percussion caps, he took it on himself to answer. 'What white man rides anywhere without a saddle?'

The three men watched as the lone stranger drew

121

closer. With his head bowed, he appeared oblivious to his surroundings.

Ewing purposefully hefted the shotgun. 'Seems like he's inviting himself to a coffee. Well I want him alive . . . unless he resists.'

His two companions moved off to the sides, their own weapons at the ready. They were pretty much prepared for anything. Yet as it turned out, because of the horse's natural instinct to move towards people, the interloper literally walked into their arms. Its rider, bloodstained and barely conscious, wasn't even aware that someone else had taken the reins.

'Get him off of there,' Ewing barked out. 'I ain't looking up to the likes of him.'

'Wahh,' was all the horseman could manage as he was roughly dragged to the ground by the big team-ster. He offered no resistance as Montoya unbuckled and removed his gunbelt.

After carefully easing down the hammers on the twelve-gauge, Ewing retrieved his coffee mug and casually tossed its contents into the prone man's face. As the hot liquid seared his flesh, that luckless indi-vidual howled in pain and quickly came to his senses. Sadly, he could draw scant comfort from the faces looming over him.

'What are you?' the trail boss barked out.

Bewildered by the abrupt turn of events, the pris-oner had to think hard for a few moments. Then he finally managed, 'W . . .Will. Will Harvey.'

His only reward was a brutal kick to the thigh, as Ewing snarled, 'I couldn't give two shits about your name. It's *what* you are that matters to me. How many steers did you steal?'

'Whaaat?'

The result of his non-compliance was another savage kick. 'You heard me. How many?'

Harvey's simple features registered a mixture of pain and confusion. He was quite plainly baffled by how these strangers could even know about such things. All he could comprehend was that he hurt bad, and wanted some respite. He couldn't have imagined that what he said next would effectively seal his fate.

'Only a couple of hundred. The sons of bitches had far more than they needed, and we had far less than we needed.' With raw anger plain to see on his interrogator's features, Harvey paused for a moment before adding, 'Why should you care, anyhu?'

'Because they're *my* goddamned steers, that's why!'

As the horrified rustler peered around for someone, anyone to come to his aid, Ewing only compounded his suffering. As though a judge addressing his court, he announced, 'This miserable wretch is fit only for hanging.'

'From what?' Sam demanded in amazement. The terrain around them was barren of anything remotely resembling a tree.

'There's more than one way to skin a cat,' Ewing responded bleakly. 'Nico, fetch me a length of rope.'

Although quite obviously unsettled by the implications, the cook nevertheless complied.

'Tie one end around the horse's neck and the other around his,' Ewing continued relentlessly.

Montoya slowly did the former, but baulked at the latter. Handing the rope to his boss, he remarked, 'Such a thing is for *you* to do, *señor.*'

The trail boss offered a fleeting smile as he recognized the other's discomfiture. 'OK. Fair enough.' Then he bent down over the condemned man.

Pure panic enveloped the young rustler. 'For pity's sake let me be. I'm shot to hell an' dying anyways.' Desperately he attempted to push Ewing away, but he was just too weak.

'Nobody steals my cattle and gets considerations,' the grim-faced executioner announced as he knotted off the rope. Then, getting to his feet, he drew and cocked his revolver and walked over to the rear of Harvey's horse. Placing the muzzle near its rump, he stated, 'Time to reach peace with your maker, Will Harvey.'

Sam suddenly raised a hand beseechingly. 'Don't you think maybe we should. . . ?'

The revolver crashed out, causing the tormented animal to rear up and then break into a dead run, dragging its pathetic burden behind it. Anything to get away from the dreadful pain. The doomed rustler never even had chance to cry out. In fact, as he disappeared into the distance, it was very doubtful whether he was still alive.

As John Ewing thoughtfully walked out a few paces, Sam and Montoya exchanged meaningful glances. 'He plays rough when he gets riled,' the former observed softly.

The cook nodded ruefully. 'And when he finally catches up with that Peck, *que dios nos ayude a todos*!'

The teamster smiled knowingly. 'I'm guessing all that had something to do with God.'

'It did, my large friend.'

'Well then, I just hope *he* gets around to visiting Kansas!'

CHAPTER TEN

Somehow, there was an urgency to the pounding hoofs that immediately set the powerfully built rancher on edge. Usually, the only time any of his men rode at that speed was on payday, when the dubious delights of a whorehouse beckoned. Which could only mean one thing.

'There's a secessionist herd on its way, just as you reckoned, Mister Stone,' the sweating ranch hand reported. 'At least three thousand head.'

At any other time Jacob Stone would have been mightily impressed that his illiterate worker could produce a word like 'secessionist', but on this occasion he suddenly had far more important matters on his mind. Standing next to the corral, seemingly oblivious to his waiting horseman, he leaned against a support post and considered his options.

In truth, he only had the one. The local 'law dog' had refused to intervene, and Stone couldn't direct his anger against Joseph McCoy and his stockyards because he had need of them, too. So all he could do was make a personal stand against the Texans and their infected cattle. A quarantine line would need to be enforced, to keep the southerners away from local animals. If he was successful, such a barrier might even force the Kansas Pacific Railroad into extending their track further west, along with McCoy's operation. Yet to achieve all this would undoubtedly involve violence, because no man relished being told where he could and could not go. Despite his belligerent demeanour, the rancher had no real taste for gunplay, but it appeared that he had no choice. So long as there was a ready market for their beef, the Texans would just keep on coming.

Stone cursed long and hard before peering up at his employee. 'Seems like it's time to break out the Winchesters. Round up as many men as you can find and send them to me. And don't spare the horse-flesh!'

The big man kept watching until his eager hand had galloped away across the rolling grassland and finally out of sight. Only then did he sigh and turn towards the impressive ranch house. He had known all along that it would come to this, but that didn't make it any the more palatable!

Because none of those men driving the herd had ever been to Kansas before, they had inadvertently drifted a little too far to the west after crossing the Arkansas River. Consequently, Peck decided to send out a couple of scouts to reconnoitre. It was about that time that they had unknowingly been spotted by

Jacob Stone's man and so, unintentionally, a sworn enemy would soon be instrumental in setting them back on the right path.

After weeks on the Chisholm Trail, every single drover was heartily sick of the sights and sounds of Longhorn cattle. They yearned for a bath, a drink, and a woman: not necessarily in that order. Due to the mysterious disappearance of the chuck wagon, their diet had consisted solely of meat, to the extent that some of the men were exhibiting signs of scurvy. Their numbers had also decreased again, because although Peck had eventually relented and sanctioned the removal of Josiah Breck's lower leg, that unfortunate had expired the following day. In truth, nobody had missed his whining and bellyaching.

It was also a sad fact that few of the Bar E hands actually gave much thought to their former employer. Far more of the arduous trail drive had taken place without John Ewing. And so, even though all of them were still wary around Vernon Peck, it could not be denied that he had done a reasonable job as trail boss. Of course, the real test would be when it came time to be paid off. And for that to happen, the cattle needed to be in Joseph 'the real' McCoy's vast stockyards!

'There's a whole heap of horsemen over yonder, boss,' reported one of the returned scouts as he pointed eastwards.

'Goddamn it all to hell!' came the entirely expected retort. 'Not more poxy rustlers?'

'Couldn't rightly say, but this lot's sure not hiding.

It's kind of like they're waiting for us.'

Peck's eyes narrowed momentarily. 'Is that so? Well then, I guess we'd better go and see what they want. Tell Reno to swing the herd over that way . . . and then round up the boys.'

Jacob Stone sat his horse and regarded the approaching horsemen with mixed feelings. After spending the winter proclaiming his intentions to all and sundry, the time had finally come to back up his fiery rhetoric. The line of armed ranch hands stretching away on either side of him provided some comfort. He also knew that many of the folks in Dickinson County supported his stand, except of course that they weren't actually present to take part. And yet, as he watched the Texans draw closer, doubt began to niggle away at him. Just who was he up against? After all, to his certain knowledge, none of his hands were gunfighters. Oh, they could blast away at snakes as well as any man, but that was a world away from facing down another *hombre* with a gun.

Stone's eyes fastened on a lean, mean looking cuss who had two Colts strapped to his waist. Surely any individual who needed two *pistolas*, must expect to waste a great deal of black powder? Or just maybe he was a very dangerous man. Something seemed to pop in the rancher's head. There really were times when too much thinking was a bad thing.

'That's close enough, fellas!' he boomed out, with every sign of great self-assurance.

Vernon Peck and the five gun thugs that accompanied him reined in about ten yards away: murderously close range if any shooting broke out. As usual it was their leader who had the words. 'Abilene must be pretty nearby if you've come out to greet us,' he remarked mildly.

Stone blinked in surprise. Was this trail bum toying with him or what? 'It's about ten miles back of us, but you won't be seeing any of it. Least ways not with them steers, anyhu.' He momentarily paused for dramatic effect, before raising his voice. 'My name is Jacob Stone, and I'm here to tell you that you're not welcome in this county.'

Peck smiled inwardly. He now knew the whereabouts of their destination, but not yet the reason for their unpopularity. 'Now why might that be, friend?'

'Because as you well know, your damn Longhorns carry tick fever with them,' the rancher retorted. 'And I ain't your friend!'

It was the Texan's turn to blink with astonishment. He genuinely had no idea what this big oaf was on about. 'Seems to me you're muddying the waters some, mister. If my cattle were diseased, how come they've walked hundreds of miles?'

Now it was Stone's turn to register disbelief. 'Because, like I just said, they're *carrying* it, not sick with it. But if they get near my animals I'll be in big trouble.' He paused and drew in a deep breath, before coming to the cruncher. 'So what you and your men are gonna do is turn to the north and keep on going.'

Peck's eyes narrowed. 'Any of you fellas badged up?'

The vigilante, which in truth was what he was, shook his head. 'I don't need no tin star. I'm protecting what's mine.'

'Uhuh,' Peck grunted. 'And what if we don't choose to move on?'

Jacob Stone patted the butt of his long gun, and replied with more confidence than he was actually feeling. 'Then we'll just have to teach you right from wrong. Us Yankees have done it before and so we can sure do it again!'

The trail boss nodded, as though everything had suddenly become very clear. He knew nothing about any tick fever, but this big Kansan obviously still harboured resentment over the recent conflict, and that was something Peck did understand.

'An' you reckon on how there's enough of you to get the job done, huh?' As he spoke, his glance ran the length of the 'quarantine' line. To his mind, just as with the Bar E drovers, none of the ranch hands looked like born killers. Bring down their leader and they'd just scatter on the wind. But then a whim came to him that appealed. It appealed very much.

Stone watched the other man's appraising glance, and he began to feel sick to his stomach. There was something reptilian about his eyes. It occurred to him that the Texan had likely seen plenty of death in his time, and had quite probably been the cause of much of it. So he was completely bemused when the makings of a smile appeared.

'We came up here to make money, not fight the war all over again,' Peck announced mildly and very unexpectedly. 'So I reckon we'll just mosey on up north a ways, like you suggested.' With that, he merely tipped his hat and turned his horse away. His startled men had no option other than to follow him back to the herd.

Jacob Stone felt as though a great weight had suddenly been lifted from him. Then elation began to flow through his taut frame. He'd actually gone and done it. Faced down the damn Texans and sent them packing. Glancing from left to right, he saw a mixture of relief and disappointment on the faces of his men. Some of them had actually naively hoped for some gunplay. Well thank God it wasn't to be!

'We'll stay awhile,' he ordered. 'Just to make sure.'

Reno regarded the fast-approaching gunhand with surprise. He would have put money on there being a bloody outcome to the confrontation. It just went to show that you couldn't always read a man.

'What do you know of tick fever?' Peck demanded.

The top hand blinked in astonishment. 'Just what we all do, I guess. That our Longhorns carry it and can pass it on to other stock. But since they're all headed for the slaughterhouse, it don't much matter. Do it?'

Peck sighed in disgust. How come he and his men seemed to be the only people who hadn't heard of the disease? 'Well it matters to those Yankees over yonder,' he retorted. 'They're fixing to stop us getting these steers to market. And the big tub in charge thinks he's still fighting the war.'

Reno's response demonstrated a surprising degree of perception. 'But you ain't taking any of that, are you?'

Peck grunted. 'Hell no. Abilene's only ten miles behind those sons of bitches. So we're gonna stampede these cows straight through them, an' keep on going. And forget about any goddamned stockyards. We'll take these animals right down the main street!'

Doubt was again beginning to assail Jacob Stone. Why hadn't those southerners begun to turn the herd? What could be taking them so long? Then, very unexpectedly, gunfire crashed out and the cattle were suddenly moving very fast ... in the wrong direction.

'Aw shit!' was his initial response. Then, quite suddenly, the rancher realized that he only had the one chance to stop them, and it was a slim one at that. 'Shoot the frontrunners!' he bellowed out.

Horrified at the prospect of remaining in front of the mad rush, not all of his men obeyed. Those that did made an impressive noise, but the quality of their fusillade was dubious, and very soon they couldn't even see because of the clouds of powder smoke they had generated.

'The hell with this!' one of them exclaimed, before turning his horse away.

'Stand fast,' Stone hollered. 'Nobody leaves 'til I say.'

'Well say it then!' an anonymous employee retorted from down the obscured line of men.

The unholy mixture of drovers and outlaws shared a common cause. They all wanted to get their beef to market. And so, stationed in a great sweeping crescent around the rear of the herd, they howled and yelled as they rode until their throats hurt. With one of Peck's men acting as teamster, that left seven of them able to add gunfire to the cacophony of noise. Their combined efforts turned the terrified Longhorns into a dangerous and unstoppable force. The couple of animals at the front that dropped with bullet wounds had no effect on the stampede.

'Yeehaa!' Reno hollered repeatedly. After weeks of gruelling travel, this final mad dash was totally exhilarating, all the more so because the varied delights of a town awaited them. The fact that he and the other Bar E drovers might well end up being cheated was lost in the pulsating excitement.

As Peck charged along on the herd's right flank he spotted a few Kansan ranch hands fleeing for their lives, and for the first time in ages he laughed out loud. So much for being kicked out of the county! Then he realized that one of them was the big blowhard who had attempted to frighten him off. With a malicious grin, he took rapid aim at Stone's horse with his right-hand Colt.

Hitting a fast-moving animal while riding one of the same called for a great deal of skill, but he pulled it off. As the revolver bucked in his hand, the escaping

134

rancher was launched from his stricken mount. Whether the man lived or died was irrelevant to Vernon Peck, because by then he was already out of pistol range, and all that concerned him now was getting his 'penny piece' for the rampaging herd. He chuckled. That town really didn't know what was about to hit it!

It was highly unlikely that many of its citizens knew that Abilene had been named from a passage in the Bible, but its meaning 'city of the plains' was very apt. Founded back in fifty-seven before the war, among seemingly endless open country, it had remained a sleepy stagecoach stop until the Kansas Pacific Railroad pushed westward, followed by the stock buyer, McCoy. Since then it had become one of the wildest settlements in the west. But even so, nothing could have prepared it for the storm of Biblical proportions that was about to hit.

It was a dissipated deadbeat by the name of Smokey Hays who first discerned the Texas 'tornado'. As normal, he had been thrown out of a saloon at some point in the night, and thereafter lay in a haze on the western edge of town. Because his skull was resting on the ground, it was vibration that first told him something was amiss. Blearily shaking his head, he peered off across the open grassland and got the shock of his life. Like everyone else in Abilene, he was used to the arrival of cattle . . . but not at this speed.

'Holy shit!' he exclaimed before jumping to his

feet. Then, most unusually for him, he made a beeline for the marshal's office.

The lawman just happened to be on his way out onto the main street when he saw the 'low-life' rushing towards him with a horrified expression on his features. 'What the hell's eating you, Smokey?' Marshal Smith enquired.

That individual came to a juddering halt and pointed a grubby finger back at the prairie. 'It'll take more than your fists to stop that lot, Marshal,' he remarked with surprising wit.

Tom 'Bear River' Smith glanced casually off to the west and froze. Less than half a mile from the city limits, a great boiling mass of Longhorns charged towards them. 'Ain't that the truth?' he muttered, coming rapidly to his senses.

Turning on his heels, the lawman raced back into his office, only to reappear a few seconds later with a double-barrelled sawn-off, cocked and ready. Pointing it in the air, he simultaneously squeezed both triggers.

Even in such a rowdy community, the massive twin discharge immediately claimed the attention of all those on the dirt thoroughfare. 'Clear the street!' Smith bellowed. Then, after pointing at the rampaging mass, he added, 'Run for your lives!'

With the stampede now plainly audible, the mostly male citizens didn't need telling twice. All of them raced for the nearest wooden building, including Smokey Hays who actually voluntarily chose the jailhouse. Unlike his unwanted companion, the marshal was thinking beyond the imminent arrival of thousands of steers. He was wondering if any of this had anything to do with that damned blowhard, Jacob Stone.

John Ewing and his two *compadres* arrived in the wake of the stampede to find a heavy-set individual groaning on the ground surrounded by half a dozen men. Nearby lay a dead horse, with what appeared to be a bullet hole in its side, and a few stray Longhorns that had somehow not got swept up in the tumult.

'What happened here?' the Texan demanded from the wagon's bench seat. In his hands he clutched the cocked sawn-off. His left shoulder was by now pretty much healed and no longer gave him any trouble.

The injured man couldn't have been that badly hurt, because he was quick to respond. 'What the hell d'you think happened?' he retorted. 'Some sharp-shooting bastard shot my horse from under me.' Then he paused for a moment to look their chuck wagon over before demanding, 'Who in Hades are you, anyhu?'

Ewing ignored the questions and instead countered with some of his own. 'This gunhand. What did he look like? Was he travelling with a herd of those beasts over yonder?'

Suspicion now mingled with pain on Stone's bluff features. He was putting two and two together and coming up with far more than he liked. To the surprise of his ranch hands, he attempted to reach for his revolver, but could only groan with pain. Whatever the heavy fall had done to him, he was currently incapable of violence. Then again, by the looks of the cold-eyed character on the wagon it was probably best that he didn't have the opportunity.

Confirming that, Ewing levelled his sawn-off and remarked, 'Tell me who shot you. Now!'

Stone sighed long and hard. 'He was a pitiless looking son of a bitch, just like you. Had two Colt Navys strapped to his waist.'

Ewing nodded, as though he had known all along. 'Well I'll tell you, mister. Those cattle belonged to me. He stole them. So when I catch up with them, I'll kill the man that shot your horse. How's that sound?'

The rancher grimaced. 'Can't argue with that, but it won't save my cattle from your Texas Tick Fever if any of your Longhorns get to run free.'

John Ewing nodded knowingly. 'Well then, I suggest you get these fellas working to keep them apart, instead of getting involved with gunfights you couldn't hope to win.' With that he lost interest in the prone rancher and turned to Sam. 'I'm gonna ride the horse over to Abilene. It's time Vern and me settled this thing. You follow on as fast as you can.'

CHAPTER ELEVEN

The vast herd struck the 'city of the plains' like an avalanche, tearing up hitching posts and knocking over barrels. Even the buildings, hastily constructed out of rough-cut timber, were not immune. Although no steer would deliberately hurl itself at a solid object, the frontrunners were propelled by the irresistible momentum of those behind. Consequently, a number of smaller structures, including privies, were literally torn to pieces. Many of the creatures found themselves on raised sidewalks, crashing into relatively flimsy doors. As support posts were knocked away, awnings tumbled down on those animals following on. Angered by the sudden invasion, a few of the more belligerent citizens actually emptied their revolvers into the cattle, with no benefit to anyone.

As the jailhouse walls trembled under repeated strikes, Smokey Hays wailed, 'Sweet Jesus, Marshal, this could be the day I die!'

Smith regarded him contemptuously. 'I couldn't be that lucky, Smokey. Besides, in my experience the only varmints to really watch out for are those that walk on two legs.' So saying, he began to reload the sawn-off with a lethal mix of scrap metal and pellets.

As more and more cattle flooded the frontier town, the many structures inevitably acted as a form of tide break, slowing down the tired animals. Some wandered off down alleys and side streets. Peck's men and the Bar E drovers had ceased firing and backed away, so pressure from the rear also eased off. Even so, it was quite some time before the herd finally ground to a halt on the far side of town. Only gradually did Abilene's citizens come up for air and reappear cautiously on the damaged sidewalks.

The settlement bore every sign of having been struck by a whirlwind, and this was only emphasized by a number of dead Longhorns lying on the main street. One of the men who had fired indiscriminately at them brandished his revolver and chuckled. 'Looks like I'll be eating steaks free for a while,' he bragged jubilantly. Conscious of a momentary interest in him, he adopted the somewhat studied pose of a big game hunter and placed a booted foot on one of the cadavers. He was still basking in his imagined glory when a large number of horsemen followed the herd into Abilene. One man in particular rode directly towards him.

'Way I see it, you owe me for five dead steers, mister,' Vernon Peck drawled softly, his voice dripping with menace. 'How's two hundred dollars American sound?'

Taken aback by such effrontery, the startled citizen

didn't take the time to evaluate the newcomer. 'For a stranger in these parts, you run your mouth kind of reckless, don't you?' he loudly queried. 'After all, I'm the one toting the gun.' It was only then that the newcomer's eyes settled on his, and for an instant he thought he'd been struck.

'Looking at all the holes in my steers, I'd say that smoke wagon of yourn is most likely empty. An' even if it wasn't, I reckon I could still draw and kill you before you even drew a bead on me. How's about we give it a go?' So saying, Peck's right hand drifted towards the corresponding Colt.

The 'cow killer' stared back at him in horrified shock. There had been something so chillingly matter of fact about the other man's words, that he realized there was a very real chance that he was about to die. It was then that he lost control of his bladder and released an embarrassing stream of urine on to the sidewalk at his feet.

The Texan favoured him with a cold smile. 'Guess that means you're gonna pay up, huh?'

From a few yards away there came the sound of an ominous double click. 'Way I see it, you owe this town a whole heap more than any two hundred dollars, mister,' Marshal Smith commented as he levelled his sawn-off. 'There's hardly a building left standing that ain't got a chunk knocked out of it.'

Peck's glance slowly shifted down the street to the lean figure sporting a badge of office on his jacket. He took in the shotgun's gaping muzzles, backed up by clear, hard eyes. Then, with a sigh, his right hand drifted back to the reins. 'This all happened for a reason, Marshal,' he responded evenly. 'Few miles back, some fella took it into his mind to stop us bringing these steers to market. Seemed to me there weren't much law in these parts, so we came anyway.'

Smith grunted, but his shotgun never wavered. 'Jacob Stone. I might have guessed. He's a local rancher fearing for the health of his stock. With no county sheriff appointed, I guess he just took matters into his own hands. But here in Abilene, I carry the law.' He let that sink in for a moment, before adding, 'I suggest you an' your men round up your cattle and move them over to the stockyards beyond the city limits. Once you and Mister McCoy have done business, we'll talk again. Fair enough?'

Vernon Peck regarded the lawman silently for a few moments before finally nodding his assent. Much as he disliked backing away from any confrontation, he recognized that it made sense not to antagonise the townsfolk any more than they already had. Not yet anyway, because for a while at least they would likely need the services of the only settlement for many miles. Slowly he turned away, and led his men down the main street.

As a peace officer of some repute, Tom Smith didn't miss much. And so it was that he noticed something very strange. Only half a dozen of the trail hands wore firearms. All the others had to settle for belt knives. That alone was enough to indicate that something was very amiss about this particular group of Texans!

*

John Ewing came up on the left flank of his wagon at a great pace, his sawn-off aimed directly at the lone teamster. Conveniently, all the firearms belonging to his employees lay in the back. A chill smile spread over unshaven features as he urged his mount to greater speed. Quickly sensing his presence, Peck's gunhand turned and blinked with shock at the sight of the shotgun.

'Who the hell are you?' he yelled over the pounding of hoofs and rattling of the conveyance. The man had obviously not got a good look at the trail boss the night Peck had shot him.

'I'm the owner of this wagon and all the cattle that went with it,' Ewing snarled. 'Now pull up pronto, before I blow you off of that seat!'

Thoroughly alarmed, the man heaved on the reins and brought the team rapidly to a halt. 'Sweet Jesus, mister. It weren't me that plugged you.'

Ewing regarded him with disdain. 'Well I think I know that, don't you? Unshuck that gunbelt and drop it in the back with the others. You've got a passenger.' So saying, he dismounted and tethered the horse to the rear of the wagon.

Trembling visibly, his prisoner did as instructed. 'You ain't gonna shoot me, are you?' he asked in strangely hushed tones.

'Well now, that kind of depends on you,' his captor retorted. He glanced over at the rooftops clearly visible ahead. 'Take me over to that town. An' if you

143

do anything, any little thing at all, to give me away, it'll be the last thing you do on this earth. Savvy?'

His throat suddenly very dry, the teamster swallowed painfully. Oh, he savvied all right!

It was only as they cleared the city limits, driving now docile cattle before them, that Peck and the others finally got a good look at their destination, and what they saw was truly amazing. Next to the Kansas Pacific railhead, a huge labyrinth of stockyards had been constructed that seemed to stretch off forever across the prairie. They would easily be able to accommodate their *mere* three thousand head. Within spitting distance of the railroad track stood an impressive three-storey building displaying the legend 'Drover's Hotel' above its main entrance. Although quite literally the end of the line, there could be no doubting that McCoy's operation was the start of something big. Apart from anything else, the cost of shipping timber from back east meant that a great deal of money had been expended.

'Well, will you look at this,' Reno muttered, his features a picture of wide-eyed wonder. It had finally dawned on him that they had actually made it. John Ewing's cattle had come to market ... except that they weren't his anymore. Perhaps it was their return to something akin to civilization that triggered it, because unaccountably the top hand was suddenly assailed by guilt. He and the others had pretty much buckled before Vernon Peck without a struggle, and only now that they were safe did it really begin to rankle. But what to do about it?

Having sent one of the stockmen in search of his boss, Peck finally dismounted near the rail track to stretch his aching limbs. It was a long time since he'd been on a train, and the prospect suddenly appealed. Take the money, cut loose from his deadbeat crew, and live on room service for a while. He smiled at the thought, and then glanced over at their wagon as it rattled towards them.

'He's taken his damn time,' he muttered to himself. Then his brow furrowed slightly. Somewhere along the way the temporary teamster had picked up a stray horse ... and there was something vaguely familiar about it. Straightening up, Peck stared at the gun thug on the bench seat. There was something decidedly odd about his demeanour.

'What the hell's up with you?' he demanded. 'Looks like someone's rammed a fence post up your ass!'

Even Vernon Peck was unprepared for what happened next. His man heaved back on the brake lever and the wagon came to a grinding halt directly in front of him. Before he could utter another word, the stock of a gun swept around in a wide arc and slammed with brutal force into the side of the teamster's skull. The luckless individual grunted and promptly fell sideways off the bench seat, to lay unmoving on the hard-packed ground with blood coating his torn flesh. Peck instinctively reached for his Colts until, for the second time that day, he found himself staring down the barrels of a twelve-gauge.

'Best tell your saddle trash not to get any fancy ideas, Vern,' Ewing snapped out. 'This crowd pleaser will cut you in half at this range. An' you'd better believe I'll do it!'

Although shaking his head in disbelief, Peck retained his wits. 'Let's not have any itchy trigger fingers, boys,' he called out, glancing around. 'I actually think he means it.' Then he settled a hard gaze on his old campaign buddy, and blew his cheeks out like a horse. 'You sure are full of surprises, John.' His eyes flitted briefly to the tethered mount. 'I suppose you had something to do with the disappearance of that goddamned chuck wagon as well? Not to mention Price and Stiles.'

Ewing nodded, but the gaping muzzles never wavered. 'And now I've come to reclaim my cattle. To that end, you and your men will drop all your weapons, and mine will recover theirs.' Then he added loudly and with noticeable bitterness. 'You hear me, Reno? If you want them, that is!'

The top hand's amazement turned swiftly to acute embarrassment. 'It sure is good to see you again, boss,' he managed.

It was at that critical moment that Joseph Geiting McCoy made a fateful appearance from the threshold of the hotel. With his sober frockcoat and flowing beard, he carried a proprietorial air that indicated both money and power. 'You men!' he bellowed with great indignation. 'I'll have no gunplay in *my* stockyards!'

Despite his experience, Ewing instinctively

146

glanced at the newcomer, and it was all the opportunity that Peck needed. Knowing that high up on a horse with nowhere to hide he made too good a target, the gunhand simultaneously slipped out of the saddle and drew his Colts. Even then he was far from safe. His opponent could have emptied both barrels at man and beast but, luckily for the gunhand, Ewing had no desire to become a horse killer. Instead that man ducked down in the wagon bed, and by so doing doomed all those present to a bloody set to.

'Reno,' the trail boss bellowed. 'You and the others need to decide whose side you're on. I'll heave your weapons off of this wagon, an' then cover you all if you choose to come for them.' He had barely spoken before gunfire erupted, and lead slammed into the body of the wagon. Splinters flew and he cursed. The timbers weren't thick enough to protect him from a direct hit. It would surely only be a matter of time before Peck and his gun thugs got lucky.

Thankfully there were no calves in the wagon bed, so Ewing had it all to himself. Crawling towards the rear, he released the catches so that the back panel dropped down on its hinges. Even as he did so a splinter painfully scored his left cheek, drawing blood. Cursing, he awkwardly got behind the assorted firearms and shovelled them onto the ground. His action didn't go unnoticed.

'Any of you goddamned drovers that side with him will get shot to pieces!' Peck hollered from behind one of the stock pens. So saying, he loosed off another shot at the wagon. The mule team tethered to it struggled desperately against the drag of the brake. 'Get around back of him,' he added, presumably to his own men.

Ewing winced as another jagged splinter struck him, this time in his left thigh. His position was becoming untenable, and he knew it.

'Sounds like a regular war going on over there,' Smokey Hays opined somewhat unnecessarily. A well-honed instinct for self-preservation meant that he had uncharacteristically remained close to the jailhouse. 'Ain't you gonna take a hand, Marshal?' he added slyly.

Tom Smith regarded him sourly. 'And ain't you got some bug juice to sup?' Then he glanced around his somewhat battered town. Various idlers were peering apprehensively towards the stockyards. First it was a stampede and now a sustained shootout. Even in a community used to outbreaks of violence, this was something else again. And yet, so long as it remained outside of the city limits it was none of his affair. As though seeking to justify his inaction, he added, 'Plain fact is, Smokey, it's outside of my jurisdiction.'

'Juris, juri . . . what the hell did you just say?' came the entirely expected response.

Nico Montoya and Sam regarded the railhead and its environs with dismay. The herd had been left to its own devices, with the humans separated into two opposing factions. Reno and the drovers far outnumbered Peck's thugs, but of course were unarmed and so totally ineffectual. Clouds of powder smoke drifted over the stockyards, where nervous animals, already owned by McCoy, shoved against the fencing in search of escape. All hell seemed to have broken loose, and it appeared as though their employer, curled up in the wagon bed, was well and truly between a rock and a hard place.

'Can you shoot as well as you cook?' the teamster queried as he drew his Remington revolver.

Montoya cleared his throat nervously. '*Madre de Dios*! This does not look good, but I will do my best for you, *mi amigo*. Just don't get my mules killed, *sí*?'

Next to the railroad track was a solid-looking ticket office, which would at least provide them with some cover. 'Take us next to that,' Sam suggested, and that was exactly what Montoya did.

What with all the noise and smoke, the outlaws were so preoccupied that the arrival of the chuck wagon didn't even register. It was only as shots rang out in the Kansas Pacific office that any of them became aware of the new threat. Then one of the thugs spun around before tumbling to the ground, blood gushing from his neck.

'Seems like you're running out of men,' Ewing taunted.

Peck spotted the chuck wagon and cursed. The 'greaser' cook had finally turned up when he was no longer needed. 'Burn those bastards out,' he ordered angrily.

'We ain't got the makings, boss,' was the entirely unsatisfactory response.

Then Mesquite Bill, always the most resistant to Peck's rule, decided that enough was enough. 'You lot can sit here making brownies all day long, but I'm gonna get into this fight!' So saying, he took a deep breath and ran for the pile of weapons.

Hot lead peppered his path, but he reached the wagon unscathed and grabbed a Henry rifle. The position of its spring-loaded tab told him that the cylindrical magazine was fully charged, which meant that he possessed more firepower than even two revolvers. Working the under-lever like a madman, he sent a stream of bullets towards Peck's gunhands.

And so, the tide began to turn.

Ewing, bleeding but no longer under sustained fire, poked his stubby shotgun over the wagon side and discharged a barrel into the back of one of his assailants. The full load tore through clothes and flesh, leaving the man writhing in agony on the hard-packed earth.

Then more and more drovers, including even the hesitant Reno, made a rush for the pile of weapons. Mesquite Bill's Henry finally dry fired, but not before his rapid shooting claimed a victim, plugged through the heart and stone dead. Vernon Peck's gang, originally twelve in number, was now reduced to three . . . and they had suddenly had enough.

'The hell with this!' one of them exclaimed, before making a dash for his horse. The others quickly followed him, leaving their former boss quite alone.

Vernon Peck, his opportunity for ill-gotten gains now depressingly non-existent, had only self-preservation on his mind. With so many guns ranged against him, any attempt to mount up and escape across open country would mean almost certain death. His only chance was to make it into Abilene, and cheat death or capture long enough to steal a horse. To that end, he promptly turned and ran into the maze of stock pens that sat between him and the settlement.

John Ewing winced painfully as he extracted the splinter from his left thigh. 'Someone get me a horse,' he bellowed. 'Any horse, to get me into town.'

Reno, suddenly eager to make amends, was the first to hand him some reins. 'Here you go, *boss.*'

Ewing's eyes narrowed momentarily, but he couldn't spare the time for sarcasm, and so merely grabbed them and mounted up. Then, without a word, he set off around the wooden enclosures. One way or another, there would be a reckoning before the day was out!

CHAPTER TWELVE

Having weaved his way through seemingly endless stock pens, Vernon Peck finally reached Abilene's main thoroughfare. Like most horsemen, he was unused to running, and so was panting heavily as he reached the hitching rail outside of the Alamo saloon. Had he possessed the time, it might have occurred to him that such a name reeked of ill omen. As it was, the fugitive was content to untether the fine-looking mustang that he found conveniently waiting there.

'I'd like to think that was your horse, mister,' Tom 'Bear River' Smith remarked loudly. 'But I'm pretty damn sure it ain't!' Standing across the street, the lawman's hard eyes were fixed on the prospective horse thief. Unlike many of his ilk, he had no love for firearms, and almost never shot to kill. Consequently, his sawn-off was aimed low, at Peck's legs. Sadly, even though seemingly ready for anything, it was a long time if ever since Smith had come up against a man with such lethal abilities.

Without any warning, and using only his opponent's voice as guidance, Peck was soon in fluid motion. Whirling around, he simultaneously side-stepped and fanned the hammer of his Colt Navy, getting two shots off with remarkable speed. It was the second one that did the damage, striking Smith in his right shoulder just as he discharged both barrels of the shotgun.

If the outlaw hadn't moved, he would have been crippled for life. As it was, most of the blast tore up hard-packed earth, but a number of lead pellets ripped into Peck's left foot, causing him to cry out. Because of the quantity of sulphurous smoke between them, neither man immediately knew how the other had fared, but even though in great pain, the gunhand instinctively went on the offensive. Nobody made him bleed and lived to brag about it!

Abandoning any attempt to grab the spooked mustang, he limped across the street towards the wounded lawman, his heart filled with malice. He was about to administer the *coup de grâce* when a number of things took his attention, requiring him to think very fast.

There was a deal of shouting around him, but he dismissed that as irrelevant. Casual onlookers were unlikely to involve themselves in bloody violence. Far more disturbing was the sight of John Ewing riding towards him from the railhead. Now there was a man on a mission!

Directly in front of Peck, the marshal was still on his feet, but was white-faced and reeling. Blood

153

coated his right shoulder and he had dropped his empty twelve-gauge. A few yards away stood the trembling figure of Smokey Hays, suddenly desperate to run away, but strangely powerless to do so. It was as though he had been mesmerised by the lethal apparition before him. Then he found himself staring at the business end of a Colt revolver, and his immediate future was definitely out of his hands.

Peck had no idea who this sack of shit was, and didn't care. '*You*, take hold of the law dog and get him into the jailhouse. *Move*, or the next chamber's for you!'

Hays didn't doubt for a second that the deadly stranger meant what he said. Hastily moving over to the swaying lawman, he grabbed him around the waist and propelled him towards his office. 'I'm awful sorry about this, Marshal,' he stammered. 'Only I really don't want to die today.'

Fighting the rising agony in his left leg, Peck hastily hustled them into the jailhouse. Momentarily glancing back, he saw John Ewing rein in outside and then he slammed the door behind him and bolted it. Limping clear of the small window, he looked down at his foot and grimaced. His well-worn boot had three distinct holes in it, through which blood was seeping. He knew that he should investigate, but there just wasn't the time.

Tom Smith lolled in a swivel chair, holding his broken shoulder and groaning. That he still lived was down to his likely usefulness, because as usual Peck had a plan. Jabbing a grubby finger in Hays's direction, he barked out, 'Tell whoever this law dog answers to that I want a fresh horse, saddled, provisioned and tethered outside, or I'll decorate the walls with his tarnal brains. Savvy?'

Hays nodded vigorously. It was blindingly obvious that he would agree to anything that got him clear of this maniac. And yet, having been roughly bundled across the threshold and back onto the street, he came face to face with another one brandishing a sawn-off.

Ewing had arrived just in time to see his enemy disappear into the jailhouse, and now this dissipated individual had come from there. 'What does he want?' he demanded, all the while ensuring that he kept the messenger between him and the law office.

The town drunk blinked in surprise. He wasn't used to being the centre of anyone's interest. 'A saddled horse outside here, or the marshal dies. He's already shot him once. I never saw anyone move so fast.' He paused momentarily before recalling the rest. 'I'm to tell the mayor.'

Ewing grunted. 'Well, you've told me instead. Now get off the street.'

Hays's watery eyes stared at him for mere seconds before he did exactly that.

'And it would behove the rest of you to follow him,' the trail boss added, in a far louder voice for the benefit of the few remaining onlookers. 'There's gonna be some dying!'

For a few moments he scrutinised the building

where his enemy had gone to ground. Then he turned on his heels and strode over to the Alamo saloon. 'Very apt,' he murmured, before pushing through the swing doors. Ignoring the many curious stares, Ewing headed straight to the rear of the large, roughly furnished room. Because there were no windows at the back, a number of kerosene lamps provided illumination for the various card games in progress. The recent shooting didn't seem to have distracted the participants, but the intruder was about to.

Striding to the nearest table, he unceremoniously seized the lamp. 'Hey, put that back, you son of a bitch,' protested one of the players. 'I've got a game going here!'

Ewing glanced down at the man's cards. 'Not from where I'm standing, mister,' he rasped, before whacking the table with his shotgun. 'Don't try making something of this. I haven't got the time and you don't need the grief.' With that, he simply turned away and walked back through the saloon carrying the flickering incendiary device.

Returning to the now deserted main street, the Texan momentarily pondered his next move. Through the window, or on the wall? With no desire to deliberately murder the local peace officer, he decided on the latter, because that way those inside would at least have some warning. Moving off to his right, he glanced regretfully at the dry goods store. The alley between it and his target was unlikely to be enough to stop the flames spreading, and he and his men would very probably have been providing it with some custom. So it was with genuine remorse that Ewing hurled the lamp at the jailhouse wall and then backed off to wait on events.

Vernon Peck heard the sound of smashing glass and 'whumph' of igniting kerosene, and shook his head with dismay. His former 'friend' had definitely rediscovered his old ruthless streak. 'That ain't very friendly, John,' he bellowed. 'Way I see it, you owe me.'

'How d'you figure that?' came the strangely disembodied response.

'Clever,' the outlaw murmured. Ewing had obviously kept moving while he spoke, to avoid being hit by an opportunistic shot. 'I let you live, that night near the camp,' he yelled back. 'An' I got your cattle through to market. Not to mention killing some rustlers for you. All that's got to be worth something.'

'Too thin, Vern. Too thin,' Ewing retorted, as he prowled around the doomed structure. 'You killed four of my men that same night, remember? Drop your guns and bring that lawman out. If you do, I'll hand you over to him to face trial. Otherwise I'll kill you for sure!'

As if to emphasize his words, the sun-dried timbers began to crackle as the flames really took hold. It was only a matter of time, and not a lot of it at that, before the interior became unbearable.

Tom Smith peered in horror at the smoke pluming through the seams in the wall. 'Unless you intend for us to burn to death, we can't stay in here much longer,' he protested.

Peck glanced down at him. Sweat poured off the outlaw's face, although at this stage that was more to do with pain from his wounded foot than heat from the fire. 'Ain't that just the truth? So here's what we're gonna do. We'll walk out of that door together, only I'll be behind you . . . an' if you're lucky you might not get cut in half by my *friend*'s shotgun.' So saying, he grabbed hold of the lawman's hair with his left hand and yanked him upright. In his right was the Colt Navy that he rammed into Smith's back.

The marshal, his right shoulder now drenched with blood, felt weak and nauseous but retained sufficient wit to realize that if he was to see the day out he had to somehow fight back. And as a former boxer he knew how to work on a man's weakness.

'OK, OK, John. You win. We're coming out,' Peck hollered. The coughing that followed was no act. Even as he prodded Smith towards the door, smoke wreathed about them. 'I'm gonna open the door now, John. You just go easy with that twelve-gauge, you hear?'

The door opened onto the street, and it was then that Smith made his move. Lifting his left leg, he slammed his boot heel down onto Peck's injured foot. He could almost feel the terrible agony that surged through his captor's body, but the lawman hadn't finished. Knowing that he had been very fortunate not to be shot in the back, he pulled clear of Peck's weakened grip. Swinging around, he then smashed his left fist with practised skill into the other man's ribs, before allowing himself to fall back out of the way.

'Finish him!' he yelled at the waiting trail boss.

Vernon Peck suddenly found himself face to face with his nemesis, but with no longer any advantage. Smith's surprise assault had resulted in his Colt pointing at the ground. Fighting the pain, he desperately tried to raise the barrel, even though he could see the gaping muzzles of Ewing's shotgun pointing at him.

'You haven't got the guts!' Peck blurted out, instinctively realizing that they were likely to be the last words he would ever utter.

The single shotgun blast took him fully in the chest, shredding his flesh and sending him careering back into the condemned jailhouse. Dead or alive, it didn't much matter. He wouldn't be coming out of that building again.

'I don't know who the hell you are, mister,' Smith gasped. 'But you'd better help me away from here. There's powder and ball a plenty in that jail, just waiting for the flames to reach.'

Ewing tossed aside his empty sawn-off and went to assist the lawman. That man had succumbed to his shoulder wound and was lying in the dirt. Once back on his feet, they moved down the street together. Only once they were well clear of the burning building did the Texan ease Smith into the rocking chair considerately placed outside of a whorehouse. It was then that he looked pointedly at the lawman's badge.

'I thought pinning that on meant you were supposed to be a *peace* officer.'

The marshal favoured him with a weak smile. 'That pus weasel was way too dangerous to be given considerations. I'm obliged to you for what you did. *Why* it happened will have to wait awhile.' As though emphasizing that last comment, a series of gunshots rattled off in the blazing building, serving to keep the street clear of idlers and gawkers.

John Ewing glanced over at it and shook his head ruefully. He had a feeling that all this mayhem was going to cost him dear, but at least he had survived the Chisholm Trail . . . and regained possession of his Longhorns. Whether he would ever want to repeat such a gruelling trek was another story entirely!